SHE SLID INTO HIS BED, WARM,
WHISPERY, AND EAGER . . .

"Is this some sort of a bribe?"

"No, Ruff." Her finger ran across his chest. Finding
just the right spot she bent and kissed him there. Then
she placed her mouth to his, those supple, caressing
lips meeting his warmly. Ruff said something which
was muffled by her lips and she drew her head away.

"If your husband comes . . ."

"He won't."

"I don't like this a bit, you know. I don't trust you."

"I know, darling." She kissed his throat and placed his
hand over her full, firm breast, and Ruff gave it up.
You can only argue so long with a lady . . .

Wild Westerns From SIGNET

RUFF JUSTICE #5

Valley of Golden Tombs

by

Warren T. Longtree

A SIGNET BOOK
NEW AMERICAN LIBRARY
TIMES MIRROR

PUBLISHER'S NOTE

This novel is a work of fiction. Names, characters, places, and incidents are either the product of the author's imagination or are used fictitiously, and any resemblance to actual persons, living or dead, events, or locales is entirely coincidental.

Copyright © 1982 by The New American Library, Inc.

The first chapter in this book appeared in *Widow Creek,* the fourth volume of this series.

SIGNET TRADEMARK REG. U.S. PAT. OFF. AND FOREIGN COUNTRIES
REGISTERED TRADEMARK—MARCA REGISTRADA
HECHO EN CHICAGO, U.S.A.

SIGNET, SIGNET CLASSICS, MENTOR, PLUME, MERIDIAN AND NAL BOOKS are published by The New American Library, Inc., 1633 Broadway, New York, New York 10019

First Printing, June, 1982

1 2 3 4 5 6 7 8 9

PRINTED IN THE UNITED STATES OF AMERICA

Valley of Golden Tombs

1

⚫━━━◆━━━⚫

SUNSET PAINTED THE walls of the adobes with a wash of pale purple. The women walked homeward from the creek, bundles of washing on their heads. Dogs yapped up the street, and a nearly white halfmoon rose hesitantly into the sky. The tall man stood at the door to the adobe house, watching night settle. The smells of cooking were in the air, the sounds of domestic arguments, of children shouting.

Dusk faded from purple to deep blue. The diamond stars flickered on one by one, and the moon took on weight and substance. The door opened behind Ruff Justice and a hand fell on his shoulder. He felt the brush of soft hair against his cheek, the weight of her head against his shoulder. She peered across his shoulder, watching day give way to night.

It was still warm. Along the creek a chorus of frogs had started their evening concert. A nighthawk dipped low over the pueblo. She was warm and strong and desirable as Ruff turned to her.

They wrapped their arms around each other and walked into the adobe, and Elena closed the door behind them. She was a dark, long-legged woman with a lot of *indio* blood. Slashing dark eyes, ripe, full mouth, heavy dark hair which fell to her waist.

1

She was not a soft woman, and she looked for strength in a man. Slowly, with the lamp in the corner burning low, Elena slipped out of her loosely fitting striped dress.

Ruff watched her admiringly, liking the thrust of her breasts, the dark prominent buds of her nipples, the flat abdomen, the long tapered legs, the businesslike hips of Elena Cruz.

Her gaze, proud and defiant, met his, and then she burst into a smile. A flashing, earthy smile. The smile of a woman who enjoyed her life, who reveled in her womanliness and in pleasing a man.

She smiled, and Ruff studied her wide white teeth, the pink cavity of her mouth, the twinkling light in her black, black eyes.

He stepped to her and put his arms around her, locking his hands together, feeling the involuntary response of the muscles of her back and hips.

"You don't kiss me?" she said teasingly, and he did. Her mouth was pliant, eager, and ripe. She kissed him lightly and then deeply again, her body going slack against him. Ruff caught the scent of cinnamon-and-yarrow soap which was Elena Cruz, and beneath it the faintly musky scent of woman.

He kissed her again, his hands resting on her naked buttocks. He kissed her small round ear through the screen of her hair, touched his lips to her throat, and then stepped back. He pulled his shirt up over his head and sat to pull off his boots.

Elena stood hip-shot, watching her long, lean man undress with frank interest. His buckskin shirt he placed over the back of a rough chair, and now he removed his pants. She smiled to herself at the whiteness of his body beneath his buckskins.

He was not heavily built, but his muscles were clearly, strongly defined. There was a puckered, jagged scar down

2

his ribcage on the left side, and below the collarbone were two silver-dollar-sized older scars.

Ruff placed his pants aside and then crossed to the lantern. Lifting the chimney, he blew out the wick. Then he walked to her in the night, taking her in his long, gentle arms.

They found their way to Elena's bed and fell into a tangle of legs and arms, their mouths searching, their hands exploring familiar, newly exciting flesh. Elena's breathing was rapid and shallow in the warm night.

Her thighs spread apart, and he felt their soft brush against his hips. He found her breasts with his mouth and his hand lay still as he kissed her gently, listening to the happy drumming of her heart.

Her hand rested on his head and stroked his dark, long hair. His head lifted and their eyes met, and in the darkness he could see her bright smile. This woman, so full of life, she who immersed herself in it, in work, in loving, smiled at him, and it was a smile which overwhelmed with its soft sensuality. Her eyes, deep in shadow, caught an errant beam of starlight, and Ruff, leaning forward, kissed her eyelids.

Her hands were on his abdomen now, slipping lower to caress and heft him, to feel the excitement in his body building to match that of her own.

She wriggled her hips slightly, sliding down in the bed until she had him positioned, and then she whispered into his ear, her words breathy, foreign, urgent.

He touched her and entered. Then, feeling strangely proud of themselves, they lay unmoving for a long minute, clinging to each other, Elena's words falling to a soft, repetitive murmur.

Ruff shifted slightly, his lips touching her throat, her breasts, her shoulders as her fingers dug into his back. He shifted once more, and the movement brought a response from Elena. She too shifted, her breath catching slightly, and Ruff nudged her again.

Elena's hips began to roll slowly, to pitch and sway. The motion was fluid, and there was a power in her hips, an animal strength which was on the verge of exploding into a wild thrusting, an overpowering, demanding response.

She held back, her pelvis moving in tight, hard circles against Ruff, her eyes half shut, lost in sensuality, her hands clutching at his shoulders.

Ruff ran his fingers along the silk of her thighs, touched her abdomen, and sank to the softness of her crotch. She moved as if he had burned her with his touch. She thrust out at him with her hips as if in anger.

But it was far from anger. Those hips began to roll and drive against Ruff, swiveling and thrusting with the hard precision of a machine, with incredible strength, demanding, devouring.

Ruff clung to her, his breath against her ear, her hips swaying, her head rolling as an eagerness rose within her, as she urged him on, urged him to lift her to a completion.

He lifted himself slightly and swayed in response to her movements, their bodies moving in perfect timing. Her hands tugged at him, dropped to her crotch to touch him as he entered, roamed his back and shoulders. Her hair was spread out against the pillow in a dark, glossy fan. She had drawn her lower lip between her teeth, and she held it there, biting down in concentration as he rocked against her, his drive growing to match the incredible pitching movement of Elena.

Her legs lifted and spread, and Ruff felt her heels rest against his buttocks, then lock around his waist as she squeezed and grappled with him. Her breathing was ragged now; her hands waved frantically and slapped at him. Her voice was pagan, her words meaningless, urgent phrases as Ruff worked against her, buried himself, split her, was met with a rush of fluid gratitude.

Their flesh was hot, perspiration-glossed in the warm night, and Elena gasped like a drowning woman, her body surging and twisting until finally, with a joyous, surprised laugh, she sat halfway up, throwing her arms around Ruff's neck before collapsing into soft surrender against the mattress.

She spoke gently, stroking Ruff's back, his thighs, answering his now-insistent thrusts with gentle pushes until she felt him go rigid in her arms, his long body tense against her yielding flesh, felt him arch his back and reach a long, trembling climax.

They lay together in the night, their hearts gentling, their breathing quieting. Elena's hands still roamed his body, her lips touching his ears, his throat, his mouth.

The night was warm and it folded itself around them like a concealing, comforting blanket, and they lay together wordlessly, in deep satisfaction, until the first crashing sound.

The boot hit the wooden door of the adobe and it cracked. Ruff Justice rolled toward the side of the bed as Elena, eyes wide, sat up in horror. She heard the door give, splintering under the weight of many bodies, and she screamed.

They poured in through the open door, backlighted by the pale moon. Justice lunged toward his Colt, which hung in its holster from the chair in the corner.

"Get him!" someone growled, and the mob of men surged forward into the room. Justice was reaching for the ivory handle of his .44, his fingers within inches of it, when the boot lashed out and took his legs from under him.

He went down in a heap, heard Elena scream again as if from a great distance, and felt the impact of a fist against his jaw.

Ruff rolled away, aware of a crowd of peons peering anxiously into the doorway, of the armed, dark men hovering over him, of the figure of Elena, sheet wound around her, her eyes wide with fright.

He rolled away, kicked out with a bare foot, and caught one of the intruders on the kneecap with his heel. The man bellowed with pain and fell back, clutching his knee.

Ruff was cornered. He picked up the small table behind him and swung it in vicious arcs, fighting back the advancing mob. There was a moment's hesitation, and then they surged forward.

The table caught one of them on the skull and he went down in a heap, but a fist arced in and caught Justice on the temple, and a boot shot out and caught him on the thigh. The table was wrenched out of his grasp, and then they were upon him with their smothering weight.

Justice fired a short right to someone's jaw, caught a fist with his eye and heard the bells began to ring in his skull, chopped out with another right which missed everything, and felt himself slammed back against the wall.

The big man was in his face, his sweaty bulk pressed against Justice, pinning him to the wall behind him. A ham-sized fist slammed into Ruff's ribcage, lifting him to his toes, driving the wind from him.

Ruff fought back the nausea, the dizzy lights which spun madly in his skull, and he kicked out, catching one of them squarely in the groin, but there were too many of them, far too many.

They had his arms and his hair. A gun barrel flashed in the moonlight and then slammed across the bridge of Ruff's nose, and he went to his knees, giving it up.

The room whirled, Elena's scream echoing endlessly as he was sucked down into the dark whirlpool at his feet, as the grim, brutal faces peered down at him and the night went explosively bright, streaked with crimson flashes before fading to dark, rubbery emptiness.

When his eyes opened again they had him by the arms and they were dragging him through the little winding streets of the pueblo. Dogs were barking at them, nipping at their heels.

Doors were quickly shut and dark eyes peered out of curtained windows. Ruff felt the blood trickling from his puffy lips. And then it was silent for a long while.

He awoke in the tiny, dirty cell of the Sonoita, Arizona, jail. He opened his eyes slowly. His cheek was pressed to the cold, hard floor of the cell. His head ached and the air was filled with the sounds of furious buzzing, like distant mad voices.

He rolled over onto his back. He was naked, stiff and in pain. He had been kicked in the ribs and there was a knot on his head. He lifted an exploring hand to finger the lump, winced as he touched it, and let his hand fall away.

He lay staring at the rough ceiling of the cell, letting the dizzy confusion settle before he tried to rise. He managed it clumsily. He stood with his weight against the wall, eyes closed as the spinning began again.

When it had passed he moved to the corner of the cell where his clothes had been thrown. Dressing was only a minor anguish.

Ruff walked to the cell door and peered out through the small, barred window. The deputy, in a huge sombrero, was tilted against the wall on a puncheon chair. He looked up sharply at Ruff.

"Well," he said, "you got what you asked for, didn't you?"

"I guess so."

Ruff turned away and walked across the cell to the window. Gripping the bars, he looked out at the small courtyard behind the jail, finding the source of the buzzing.

A yellow-flowering mimosa tree was alive with bees.

7

One of them flew into the cell, angrily buzzing against the wall before it returned to the tree, flying arrow-straight past Ruff's eyes.

He walked to the cot which hung from rusty iron chains and sat down, holding his head. *You got what you asked for.* The bees hummed away the day in the tree outside the window.

They came for him the following morning, and there was a trial of sorts. The huge, mustached judge sat fanning himself as the prosecutor, who was also the sheriff, read the list of complaints against Señor Ruff Justice. There was no jury—no point in disrupting the workday of twelve good villagers. The judge heard the case himself, deliberated himself, and himself passed the sentence.

"Twelve years in the territorial prison at Tucson, where you will have ample time to reflect upon the evil of your ways."

"That does seem like ample time, Your Honor," Justice said, but there was no humor in those cold blue eyes.

The judge glared at him for a moment, then waved a hand. Lifting his massive bulk from the chair, he departed for the cantina next door.

Justice was shackled ankles and wrists, and seated in the back of an oxcart driven by the sheriff's slope-shoul-dered deputy. The sheriff himself rode behind the cart, shotgun in his hands, an expression of triumphant righteousness on his dark face.

They passed a knot of dirty, barefoot kids who broke off their game long enough to hurl rocks at the prisoner, and then they were out of Sonoita, jolting along the rough desert road toward Tucson. Justice had had only a single fleeting glance at the dark-eyed woman in the striped shawl who stood in the door to the adobe, watching after him.

2

THE PRISON WAS a low stone building surrounded by an adobe wall and built in the rough shape of a pentagon. There was a watchtower at each corner of the wall. Farther out, barbed wire had been strung tautly. Parallel with the wire were twelve-foot trenches, one on either side of the wire.

It could have been worse, Ruff was thinking. He wasn't sure how, but it seemed it could have been worse. The sheriff halted the oxcart at the high frame-and-barbed-wire gates and handed over the judge's commitment papers to a very tough and very bored-appearing guard, who glanced at them, handed them back, and then turned and waved to his counterpart on the other side of the gate. The second guard unlocked the entrance and the oxcart rolled through.

Justice could see gangs of trusties wearing drab green uniforms at work out on the desert between the wire and the prison proper. Two mounted guards with Winchesters watched as the barren ground was picked clean of rocks, which were thrown into a wagon to be carted back to the prison, presumably to be used in the construction of still more buildings—or maybe it was a job invented only to keep the prisoners busy.

Eyes flickered toward the oxcart, and now and then a blank, gray face turned to watch.

At the prison proper they passed through another gate, this one of iron-strapped oak, and into a courtyard.

"This is home, Mr. Justice," the sheriff said without sarcasm. "Hope it suits you."

"I won't be here long," Ruff said, hopping down, his ankle chains clanging.

"Yeah, that's what they all say, isn't it?" the deputy asked over his shoulder. Ruff only shrugged. The reception committee was on the way.

A burly man with a walrus mustache and thick sideburns strode toward the cart. Siding him were two uniformed men, both seemingly unarmed, but Ruff would have bet they had a truncheon or maybe brass knuckles stowed in their pockets.

None of them changed expression as they looked Justice over, shook hands with the sheriff, and received the commitment papers.

"There's coffee if you men would like some," the man in the suit told the sheriff.

"Thank you, sir," the sheriff answered, "but we'll be getting back to Sonoita." He looked around him, obviously not liking the place much. The deputy mopped his brow with his sleeve. It was hot.

"You will be staying, won't you, Mr. Justice?" the man in the suit asked. He was smiling sardonically.

"Does that pass for humor around here?" Ruff asked.

"Yes." The smile straightened out, and Ruff saw a glint in the brown eyes. This was not a nice man. "Goodbye, sheriff," he said. The sheriff waved a hand and turned his horse. The oxcart rattled along after him, and they passed through the gate and out onto the desert. The gate slammed shut and Ruff felt suddenly vulnerable.

"My name is Forbes," the man in the suit said. "Deputy Warden Forbes."

"Happy to meet you."

"If you are, you're a damned fool," Forbes snapped.

"That's been said," Ruff answered.

Forbes looked the tall man up and down, taking in the buckskins, the long hair which curled down across Ruff's shoulders, the black mustache which drooped below his jawline. That and those cold, cold blue eyes. Then he nodded as if making up his mind.

"We've a hardcase here, Harry," Forbes said to one of the guards.

"Looks like it." Without any further prompting, Harry stepped in, stamped down hard on Ruff's instep, and then slammed a sickening punch into his belly. When Ruff doubled up from that, Harry came up with a knee. The knee caught Ruff flush on the chin, cracking his teeth together. He fell back heavily and landed hard, his skull banging against the ground.

Harry bent over him and expressionlessly helped him to his feet. Forbes wasn't smiling now, but he was enjoying it, Ruff could tell.

Now the deputy warden stepped nearer, and he spoke in a hiss.

"I am Deputy Warden Forbes. You will address me at all times as 'sir.' You will not speak to me unless spoken to. You will address the guards as 'sir' at all times, and you will accomplish whatever task they give you immediately, without question. Do you understand that, Mr. Ruffin T. Justice?"

Ruff's eyes were cold. He nodded at Forbes and then with a smile replied, "Sure."

Forbes went rigid. His fist clenched and unclenched. Harry stepped in and lowered the boom. A big fist caught Ruff under the ear, and he went down again. He lay there curled up defensively as Harry kicked him three times, finding the kidneys. Pain shot through Ruff and it felt as if the top of his head was going to blow off.

"You call the deputy warden '*sir*'!" Forbes said. A driving boot toe punctuated the order. "You will call me '*sir*,' hardcase." Panting, Harry was pulled back, and slowly Ruff got to his hands and knees, his chains tangled into a knot.

He rose, throwing back his head to gasp for air. Forbes's chest was rising and falling wildly.

"Do you understand us, Mr. Justice?" he asked, and his voice cracked with emotion.

"Yes . . . Forbes," Ruff answered. Harry's hand went up, but before it could fall a voice boomed out.

"Forbes!"

The tall man with silver hair was striding across the yard. Harry stepped back and stood rigidly aside. Forbes swallowed a curse and tried on an ineffective smile. Ruff stood weaving, blood trickling from his nostrils and lips.

"What is this?" the tall man asked.

"A new prisoner." Forbes handed over the commitment papers. "He's a smart-ass, sir."

The tall man glanced at the papers and put them away in his hip pocket. "Can't you even wait until we have them in uniform, Forbes?" he asked almost with weariness.

"He won't learn any sooner, sir," Forbes said.

"Bring him up to my office," the tall man said.

"Yes, warden," Harry answered.

"And clean him up!" The warden turned and walked away. Forbes muttered another curse. Harry's partner produced a filthy towel from somewhere and ran it over Ruff's face, removing the blood. Then, with a guard on each arm, the chains clanking as he walked, he was guided into a stone building, down a corridor where their footsteps echoed, and into a pleasantly decorated room. A thin young man at the desk looked up and nodded his head toward an inner door.

The warden was at his desk. "You can leave, Hammerschmidt," he said to the guard. "Yates." Both guards looked to Forbes, who nodded permission. Then they turned and went out, closing the heavy door behind them.

Ruff Justice stood looking at the warden, who was scratching his signature onto something, at the walls, which were paneled roughly, at the various Indian artifacts—hatchets, war bonnets, shields, and lances—which decorated the room. He looked at Forbes, noticing the narrowed eyes, the twitching of the jaw muscle beneath the sunburned, taut skin.

"Now then," the warden said, pushing his papers aside. "Let's do this right. I am George Donovan, warden of this prison. This is my deputy warden, Oliver Forbes. You are . . ." He looked at the commitment papers. "Ruffin T. Justice. Let's see . . . assault, arson, threatening an officer of the law, displaying a deadly weapon in a threatening manner, inciting to riot!" The warden shook his head without glancing up.

"Were you drunk or what?" Donovan wanted to know.

"I don't drink," Justice said as if that answered it all.

"Then I don't understand this wild spree of yours. A man with your record." He looked at the papers before him again. "A lot of army time. Civilian scout after the war. Dakota, Kansas, Colorado. Why, Mr. Justice?" Donovan asked. "Why try to singlehandedly tear a little town apart?"

"I really can't see that it matters a damn now, warden," Ruff answered.

"Answer the question," Forbes said.

"I just did," Ruff said thinly.

"Damn you, Justice!"

"Settle down, Oliver," the warden said, waving a limp hand. "It doesn't matter now, he's right." He shifted his gaze back to Justice. "I just like to know about my prisoners, Mr. Justice. I like to think I'm fair, and I try to start evaluating men from the moment they step through that door. Down the road when the possibility of parole exists, I like to have the facts to put before the board. To tell you the truth, Justice," he said, leaning back, "you haven't impressed me favorably."

Justice only shrugged. Forbes shook his head in disgust. "See what I mean, warden?"

"I'm beginning to." The warden rose. "You're going to have to work on that attitude of yours, Justice," he said, "or I'm afraid you'll be with us a long, long time."

"And if I kiss your fanny how soon can I get out?"

Donovan stared at him for a long time, then, letting a hand flutter in the air in dismissal, he turned away. "Process him, Forbes."

Forbes shoved Justice toward the door and through the outer office. Once in the corridor, Forbes slammed Ruff up against the stone wall and hissed, "You think you're tough, don't you? Let me tell you, you haven't even seen tough! You haven't dreamed of it. We've got some of your kind in here, and we know how to handle them."

Harry and Yates had reappeared from somewhere, and Forbes, after one long last glare, shoved Ruff into their arms. "Take him through," the deputy warden said, and Harry smiled with grim satisfaction.

"Yes, sir."

He didn't wait until Forbes was out of sight before he buried his kneecap in Ruff's groin.

Justice folded up, his stomach flipping over, pain setting off flashing pinwheels behind his eyes. He retched, held it back, and, taking slow, deep breaths, straightened up again.

"We got fast learners and slow learners in here," Harry said. "The fast learners get hurt a hell of a lot less."

Ruff couldn't speak to answer the guard just then. Harry grinned toothlessly and, gripping Justice by the shoulder, turned him and guided him down the empty corridor. From somewhere beyond the walls the sound of a bell clanging reached Ruff's ears.

They entered a small, gray room where a trusty with white hair and one arm was scrubbing the stone floor. Another prisoner in the same drab green uniform rose quickly behind a battered desk. Harry produced a key and removed Ruff's shackles.

"Fresh meat," Harry said. "Strip him and wash him down—and watch yourself."

The trusty, of middle years with close-cropped red hair, nodded and said, "Follow me." Ruff hesitated, was kicked in the back of his leg by Harry Hammerschmidt, and hobbled forward.

Entering a tiny, windowless room, the trusty said, "Strip 'em off."

Ruff did so, the trusty watching. "It ain't so bad once you're settled in," he said in a lowered voice. "Only don't give Harry H. any trouble. He'll break your back for you, friend."

"He'll try," Ruff said coldly. The trusty only sighed. "Through here."

Ruff followed him into a second room. There was a drain set in the floor and a tank made from an old barrel suspended overhead. The trusty tossed a heavy bar of yellow lye soap to Ruff. "I got to go up above," he said. Ruff didn't reply.

He stood under the barrel while the trusty released a thin trickle of cold water. Ruff scrubbed down with the soap, discovering that it was a little tougher to bend over than it had been before entering the prison. Harry not only enjoyed his work, he was good at it.

"Done?"

Ruff nodded and the trusty yanked the wire, letting a little more water shower down. Clambering down, he produced a towel, which Ruff took.

They went out through a different door and entered a

storeroom beyond it. A shriveled-up trusty stared without interest from behind wire mesh. He looked Ruff up and down, turned, and disappeared for a few minutes. Returning, he opened a gate in the screen and shoved out a starched green uniform.

"Put 'em on," he advised.

Ruff did so silently. The clothing scratched. The shirt was stiff as cardboard.

"Come on."

Ruff was led out another door into a room where Harry and Yates waited, backs against the wall. Ruff saw with relief that his boots were waiting for him. That much was right anyway. He sat down on a wooden bench and tugged them on under the watchful gaze of Harry H.

Standing, he was escorted down a corridor to an iron-barred doorway. A turnkey let them through without speaking. It was a minute before a big man, sleeves rolled up, came to meet them.

"Here's one for your block, Walt," Harry said. "He's one of them spit-in-your-eye types."

"Oh, he is, is he?" Walt said in a monotone. He was thickly built, with sad, pouched eyes. He seemed weary and he moved heavily. Ruff couldn't detect any malice in Walt's expression.

"I'll line him in," Walt said, and Harry nodded, casting one last glance at Ruff Justice. The turnkey silently let Harry H. and Yates out, and Ruff was left facing the big man.

"Come along," Walt said. He ambled off down a hallway. Passing through another door, they came to the cell block proper. Long rows of wooden doors with iron-grated windows faced each other across the cold stone corridor. Here and there a hand was visible, clinging to the grate. Shadowed faces peered out as they passed down the corridor.

"You won't spend a lot of time in here," Walt told him

in the same monotone. "Mostly you'll be working. Unless
. . ." He looked quickly at Ruff, perhaps recalling Harry
H.'s warning. "Unless you can't get along. Then you'll be
spending a lot of time in the lockup. There's worse than
this too," he said, stopping suddenly so that Ruff nearly
walked into him. "Stay clean, Justice. This isn't a nice
place to be. It isn't a nice job I've got here, but I can
tolerate it. I have for a long while. Let me say this—I'm
no Harry Hammerschmidt, but I don't care much for un-
necessary trouble. It makes my job a lot less tolerable. I
don't like that." He fixed those mournful eyes on Ruff
and told him once, "I can be rough if I have to be."

Ruff, studying the man, believed it.

Walt took his key ring from his belt and opened one of
the cells. Ruff was aware of a narrow, watching figure in
the corner of the dark room.

"Stand back, Rackets, officer entering the cell!"

The slender figure scooted to the farthest corner, and
Walt motioned Justice in ahead of him.

Now by the light which seeped through a high, narrow
window Ruff could make out the hatchet-nosed, greasy-
haired prisoner who was to be his cellmate. He watched
him warily with animal eyes, a smirk on his lips.

"This is Rackets," Walt said. "Rackets, Ruff Justice.
He's your bunkmate. Show him the ropes."

As he spoke, Walt moved around the cell, lifting pillows, patting the blankets of the two opposing bunks,
peering into the small wooden chest in the corner. Rackets, his back to the wall, hands spread against it, watched,
his glance occasionally shuttling to Ruff Justice.

"Rackets'll show you what you need to know," Walt
said. He started out the door and then halted. Without
turning, he said to Ruff, "Keep your head down, boy, or
you're liable to have someone take it off."

Then the door closed with a bang. Ruff heard the key

turn in the lock. He stood in the middle of the room, watching Rackets. The small man grinned nervously.

"That's your bunk," he said in what was nearly a falsetto.

Ruff nodded. Seating himself on the bed, hands clasped, he watched Rackets. He came out of the corner stealthily, and Ruff noticed he had a game leg.

"What'd they hang on you?" Rackets asked. Ruff didn't answer. "Me, they say I poisoned my old lady. But I didn't. I'm innocent, but no one listens."

"Tough."

Rackets' eyes narrowed and he shuffled nearer to Ruff. "You're a hardcase, ain't you? Good. Maybe you and me can stick together."

Ruff nodded, looking away from Rackets. He let his eyes survey the room, the solid stone walls, the high, barred window, the bunks and the chamberpot, the washbasin and two wooden trunks. Home. He stood, and Rackets practically fell backing away from him. He crouched, greasy hair in his eyes, watching Ruff as he circled the room.

"You can't break out of this joint," Rackets said. Ruff's head turned slowly toward him. The small man was grinning. "Surprised I know what you're thinking? All the new meat thinks about busting out when they get their first smell of this hole. But you can't crack this pen, Justice. No one ever has."

"Anybody try?"

"All the time," Rackets said with a slippery smile. "That's how I got this." He gripped his bad leg. "Harry H. busted it for me."

"Tough."

"Yeah." Rackets sat on his bunk, keeping his thoughts to himself. From somewhere a bell clanged, and Rackets, coming to his feet, said, "That's us. Suppertime."

A guard was strolling down the hall, rapping on the

doors with a baton and then opening them. At each door he called out, "Mealtime. Orderly lineup!"

When their own door swung open, Ruff followed Rackets out. Up and down the corridor men stood with their backs to the wall. One blue-uniformed guard stood at each end of the corridor with a carbine in hand while the third unlocked the cells.

Ruff's eyes flickered up and down the hall, studying the faces. The one he was looking for wasn't there, but then he wasn't supposed to be. On command all the prisoners turned right and shuffled forward, silently filing through the door.

They went out into a yard and crossed it to a low wooden building. Ruff could smell the food cooking. It wasn't exactly enticing. No one spoke as they entered the dining hall. They were just long lines of mute green men. They sat to the tables on long benches, in the order they were in.

No one spoke. Three guards were posted around the room on platforms. The meal was a tasteless lumpy gruel served from huge kettles, spooned into tin bowls which were passed from hand to hand down the long table. Ruff ate quickly, as they all did. It was best to get it down before you had the time to think much about what you were eating.

After the meal it was recreation time. That meant that you were allowed to stand around in the yard and speak. Ruff stood near a wall with Rackets tenaciously hanging on. Ruff studied all the faces in the yard, still not finding the one he was looking for.

Beyond a six-strand wire fence there were other buildings. Low, silent, mean-looking affairs.

"That's the punishment barracks," Rackets told him, catching Ruff's interest. "You don't want to go there. Harry H. does what he wants once you're there. Warden Donovan can't protect 'em."

"Why not?"

Rackets shrugged. "Everyone knows they're hardcases. All they got to do is say he was assaulting a guard, that's why he's all beat up. Some of 'em assault a hell of a lot of guards," the small man said.

Ruff nodded thoughtfully. Then as Rackets watched he got down on the ground and started doing push-ups. Heads turned to study him. Snickers were exchanged. Ruff ran through fifty push-ups and turned, seating himself on the ground.

"What are you doing that for?" Rackets asked.

If the man didn't know there was no point in telling him. Justice had no intention of turning to mush in here. He lay back, extending his arms over his head. Then he sat up, touching his toes. He repeated that fifty times. Rising, he asked, "All right to take a walk around the yard?"

"Yeah, sure." Rackets looked at him as if he were nuts.

"Want to come?"

Rackets shrugged and followed after the long-striding Ruff Justice. Ruff never slowed down, and Rackets, on his bad leg, had difficulty in keeping up. The little man was panting by the time they reached the side of the yard that fronted the punishment barracks.

There Ruff slowed, studying the layout of the place, searching the dark eyes of the barred windows. "Say," Rackets panted, "are you going to do this every day?"

"Every chance I get," Ruff replied. With a smile he said, "Let's pick it up a little, all right?"

He broke into a jog, and Rackets, after a grunt of protest, followed, running crookedly on his game leg.

It was a quarter of a mile around, and when they reached the starting point Rackets stood panting, supporting himself with arms braced against his knees as he drew in great lungfuls of breath.

"You're crazy," he puffed.

"I'm going again," Ruff said. "How about it?"

Rackets shook his head wearily, and without another word, Ruff turned and started off at a jog, moving past the eyes of the other convicts, who goggled, smirked, and laughed out loud at the tall, long-haired prisoner who was running, running—and getting nowhere.

It couldn't have bothered Justice less. This time he didn't slow down when passing the punishment barracks, yet his eyes were moving all the time. It would pose a problem to get out of there. Getting in should be a cinch.

3

---◆▶◈◀◆---

"PILE OUT!" CRUTCHFIELD hollered, and the prisoners obeyed. They slipped from the heavy, weathered wagon and formed themselves into a rough rank while Crutchfield, a thin, nervous man, and two other guards watched.

Rackets and a fat prisoner named Sticks handed down the tools. Ruff stood silently in ranks, watching the hectic movements of Rackets, the nervous faces of the guards, the frozen expressions of the prisoners. "Never smile," Rackets had told him once. "It makes them think you're up to something."

The sun was a white ball of heat high in the desert sky. Sweat trickled down Ruff's neck and chest. He was near the end of the rank, waiting while Rackets handed out the tools. He made use of the time to study the terrain.

They had been carted out to within fifty feet of the perimeter fence. Here greasewood had begun to grow waist-high, and they were to clear it. It had nothing to do with beautification. The watchtower guards needed a clear line of sight anywhere on the flats. The brush was just high enough to conceal a man.

"Here." Ruff looked up and took the heavy hoe. He returned his attention to the fence.

You came first to a trench twelve feet deep and eight wide, then the tangle of barbed wire itself, then another

22

trench, just as deep. A man—saying he could make it this far across the flats without being shot—could probably leap the first trench on the run. But then what? Over or through the wire and try jumping the second ditch from a standing start without attracting attention? Not likely. But there had to be a way. When the time came he would have to have a plan and a good one, or this would all be wasted.

"What're you? Sleeping?" Crutchfield barked at Ruff, and Justice shook his head. He got to work, chopping at the heavy brush while the sun beat down on his back. The greasewood was much too heavy for a hoe, but the guards had been reluctant to hand over axes.

They did the best they could. Ruff chopped brush, stacked it aside to be carried back to the wagon by other hands, and thought.

If a man tumbled into one of those ditches, could he crawl back up? And what about the dogs? Ruff had seen their tracks everywhere, though he hadn't caught sight of a dog yet. Apparently they were only out at night. Did that mean daytime, unlikely as it was, would be best? He worked nearer the fence.

Crutchfield stood guard as a trusty, old and withered, probably an Indian, laid two long planks across the ditch on this side of the wire. Ruff's eyebrows lifted and he worked with furious concentration, glancing only occasionally, innocuously, at the activity near the fence.

The Indian was tightening the fencing, hammering staples into the posts under Crutchfield's watchful eye. The fat man, Sticks, was hobbling that way with two huge coils of shiny new wire.

The wire didn't hold Ruff's attention, but something in Sticks' pocket did. Wire cutters, used to cut the wire ties around the new coils. Ruff turned his face down and worked busily.

Sticks passed close, so near that Ruff could hear his labored breathing, see the perspiration glistening on his pink face. Still it wasn't near enough.

Sticks crossed the plank bridge warily, nervously looking downward. He dropped the coils of wire and returned under Crutchfield's baleful gaze.

Ruff worked himself nearer to the ditch, his hoe rising and falling methodically.

"What the hell's up?"

Ruff lifted his eyes to see Rackets picking up an armful of brush. His dark eyes were narrow and suspicious. Ruff shook his head slightly and turned his back.

Rackets, burdened with an armload of brush, turned and walked back toward the wagon. Ruff's hoe fell in an easy rhythm. Sticks, staggering under the load of two more coils of wire, was returning toward the plank bridge. Ruff was alerted by his heavy breathing.

Sticks was to him and then nearly by him when Ruff's hoe somehow got tangled with Sticks' ankles and the big man went down like a felled redwood. He hit the ground face first and bellowed with pain as the wire he carried bit into his shoulders and hands.

"Are you all right?" Ruff was to him first.

"You tripped me, you bastard!" Sticks whined.

"Don't be ridiculous. You've got to watch where you're going." He put a hand under Sticks to help him up, saw Crutchfield, rifle held high, rushing toward them.

"What's going on here?" the guard shouted.

"He fell, that's all. Take it easy," Ruff said, backing away, hands held high.

"You clumsy ox," Crutchfield muttered. He watched as Sticks untangled himself and came ponderously to his feet. "You all right?"

"Yes." Sticks was still panting. Blood trickled from one of the numerous tears in his shirt. "It wasn't my fault, he—"

"Get moving. Both of you get back to work!" Crutchfield said, spinning away on a bootheel. Ruff shrugged apologetically and got back to his hoeing.

Sticks crossed the plank bridge, dropped his rolls of wire, and patted his pocket for his snips. Gone! He must have dropped them when he fell, or . . . Crutchfield was watching him through narrowed eyes.

Sticks turned and bent over the wire, concealing the fact that he was unfastening the stiff retaining wire with his fingers. Sticks was an old hand, and he was damned if he was going to admit to the guard that he had lost some wire cutters. Wire cutters, by God! He had hopes of a parole within the next year, and he wasn't going to give them any ammunition to use against him.

"I lost the wire cutters," he could hear himself saying.

"Took them, you mean," the response would be. "And what were you planning to do with wire cutters, Sticks?" The hell with that.

The stiff ends of the wire bit at his fingers, and Sticks mumbled a curse. It came to him suddenly. That tall man with the mustache, the new prisoner! He turned to look at Justice, but the expression he saw was all innocence.

Rackets picked up another armload of brush. Under his breath he said, "You worry me, Justice. You really do." Ruff shifted his innocent expression to Rackets. "Jesus," the little man muttered, walking away.

They ate lunch in the shade of the wagon. Gruel, augmented by one small apple apiece. They had fifteen minutes to doze in the dry hot shade before Crutchfield blew a whistle.

Sticks walked close to Ruff Justice as they scraped their plates into a garbage can—which, someone insisted, would be reheated for the next meal.

"Give 'em back," Sticks hissed. Ruff looked blandly at the big man.

"What?"

"You know what!" He looked down toward Crutch-field. "Give 'em back."

"You've had too much sun, pal." Ruff nodded and walked away. Sticks started after him, then thought better of it. The tall man had a hard look about him. Wagging his head like an ox, Sticks tossed his dirty utensils into a box and went back to work.

The sun beat down for hour after hour. One man dropped out, going flat on his face, the sun having beaten him. The others slowed their pace reflexively. Crutchfield was finished with the fence-repair work. The planks were drawn back.

Ruff was working shoulder to shoulder with a big-shouldered, slim-hipped black man. Ruff looked behind him, straightened up, and said almost conversationally, "Is that a rattler?"

The black man jumped back, and he shouted, "Where? Where!"

A second prisoner heard the shouting and asked, "What is it?"

"Goddam rattler!"

There was a quick scurrying away from the area. Crutchfield, face red, mouth damning prisoners present, past, and future, came on the run.

"What's the matter!"

"A big rattler. Someone saw a big snake."

"You got hoes, don't you?" Crutchfield asked angrily. "Hit it!" Nevertheless he came closer, taking an intense look. He saw nothing but piles of brush. Poking at these with his rifle barrel while the prisoners stood back, his attention was distracted.

Ruff Justice, even nearer the trench now, dipped into his pocket, came up with something metallic, and with a single fluid motion flipped it across the ditch to land near an especially crooked fence pole.

"There ain't no damned snake here," Crutchfield growled. "Get back to work."

Ruff obliged, a thin smile playing on his lips. The high-pitched voice at his shoulder belonged to Rackets. "You do worry me, tall man. You really do."

That night in their cold, dark cell Ruff lay, hands behind his head, staring at the high, narrow window where thin blue starlight shone. Now and then someone coughed or snored, but for the most part it was silent in the cell block. Men were weary from the day's work. They sought escape in their bright, lying dreams.

"You really are going to try it, aren't you?" Rackets asked from out of the darkness. When Ruff didn't answer he asked again, "You really are going to try a breakout?"

Ruff grunted noncommittally.

There was a small scuttling sound and then the weight of Rackets' body against Ruff's bed. Ruff rolled his head that way. The little man's eyes were bright in the starlight.

"You got to take me with you!" he whispered.

"Who says I'm going?"

"I saw you. I saw you trip Sticks. I saw you toss those wire cutters."

"It was just a little joke on the fat man." Ruff yawned. "I just wanted to get his goat a little."

"You've got to take me," Rackets said with what was nearly desperation.

"Yeah?" Ruff's head lifted from the pillow. "After last time? You want to lose your good leg?"

"Is that it? You think I can't keep up?"

"That's not it."

"Why?" he demanded. The question was too loud, and he looked nervously toward the door. "Why?"

"I told you."

"And I didn't believe you!" Rackets gripped Justice's arm and squeezed. He sensed something then, some unspoken threat. This was a man who did not wish to be touched. Rackets' hand slid away.

"Maybe," Ruff said slowly. "Maybe, if we're still together."

"We will be. I'll stick with you." Rackets' hair hung in his eyes. He was grinning. He backed away toward his bunk. "We'll make it. I can read you, Justice. You're hard, harder than any of 'em. We'll get out."

"Maybe," Ruff repeated. Then he closed his eyes, leaving Rackets to his dreams.

In the morning Harry H. and Walt came through the cell block. Beds were torn apart, men stripped. They told no one what they were looking for, but Ruff had a fair idea. They didn't find it.

"Damn," Rackets said respectfully after the search team had gone. "You pulled that off. Anybody else would've kept those snips with 'em. Damn!" His admiration was nearly embarrassing. Ruff tucked his shirt in and stood beside the window patiently waiting for breakfast.

Rackets wanted to break out, did he? Let him have the dream for a few hours. Let him believe that Ruff and he were inseparable, bound to escape. Ruff had other plans. It was time to step things up. Time to move out.

Getting in will be the easy part, Ruff. But for the rest of it—I hate to ask you to put yourself in the spot you'll be in. There've been too many stories leaking out of that prison. Men who've been broken in that punishment barracks. Shattered and smashed.

There was no point in thinking about it anymore. He had taken on the job, and there was no backing out. It was only a matter of how, or maybe of who.

He stayed low for the next day or so. The first day found him back on the desert, chopping brush. The second brought a bit of unexpected luck—he was assigned to the blacksmith, whose regular helper had dropped some stock on his foot, breaking it.

"Just keep that furnace stoked," the smith had told him. He was burly and tough-looking. Ruff did as he was told. The heat was incredible. It was well over a hundred outside and he was standing inside where there was no breeze, next to the forge, which blazed with heat. It was a good time for it.

Still Ruff waited. He had been thinking about the opportunity he had here, and when the smith, stripping off his leather apron, went out on some business, Ruff moved quickly.

He had already selected the stock he wanted to use, and he sawed two four-inch lengths of round iron from it. Each length of stock he then placed in the vise, hammering a ninety-degree angle on either end.

Watching the door, Ruff hurriedly heated and flattened the ends of one of these, leaving the other round. He wasn't sure exactly what he would need.

Finished, he cooled the iron bars and slipped them into his boot top. The blacksmith still had not returned, and Ruff took a minute to prepare himself a little further.

Taking a hand towel, he tore it into strips and packed the cloth around his teeth—not that he was vain, but he had grown accustomed to those teeth over the years. It would be a shame to lose them all.

He had just finished poking the cloth into his jaw when the smith returned. Ruff straightened up and turned to lounge insolently against the wooden wall.

"What the hell are you doing?" the smith demanded. "That damn fire is nearly burned out. Pack some coal into it."

"Do it yourself, fat man," Ruff growled, turning away.

"Did I hear you right, hardcase?" the smith exploded. He stepped nearer, his huge bulk casting a shadow against the wall. His voice dropped to a menacing hiss. "You know what trouble I can make for you by reporting insubordination?"

Ruff waved a hand, "Do what you want to do, fat man. Me, I'm quitting." He walked to a bucket, upturned it, and sat down.

The smith was quivering with anger now. "If you know what's good for you, you'll get up now and get to it. I'll forget this."

"You go to flaming hell," Ruff said.

For a big man the smith could move quickly. He was to Ruff in three steps and his chunky leg swung out, kicking the bucket from under Ruff.

Justice nearly went over with it, gathered himself, and came to his feet, expecting what happened next—he just didn't expect it to be that tough.

The big man could hit, and as Ruff came to his feet the smith looped a right hand which caught Ruff on the ear. A crushing blow, it spun Ruff's head half around and banged him into the wall.

The smith waded in, throwing lefts and rights, catching Ruff on chest, shoulders, head. It was artless, but the blows were punishingly effective. Ruff covered up and tried to duck away, but the smith came up with a left uppercut which seemed to have his weight and the weight of two other men behind it. Ruff's head snapped back and slammed into the wall behind him.

He kicked out, gained some room to work, and laid into the smith. Three short, sharp jabs backed the smith up and Ruff connected with a good right which caught the big man below the ear.

He shrugged the blows off. Coming straight in, his chin tucked, the smith landed three hard body shots. Ruff thought a rib cracked. The breath rushed out of his body and the lights went on in his head—he was beginning to wonder about the wisdom of this.

But there was an easy way out, and Ruff took it now. He winged a wild right at the smith's head, connecting glancingly, and walked into a solid countering punch.

Ruff went down in a heap, watching the smith through the slits between his eyelids. For a moment it looked like the big man was going for his sledge hammer—in that case Ruff would have come to his feet, and fast. But he decided against it, it seemed. Ruff heard him panting heavily, saw him bending over at the waist, sucking the air into his lungs. Then, with a last look at Justice, he walked to the door and hollered out.

Ruff closed his eyes and listened to the voices.

"The son of a bitch jumped me. I had to lay him out."

"I heard about this one. Thinks he's a hardcase. Don't worry about it, Hank."

Then the guard's toe was driven savagely into Ruff's ribs. He gasped with the pain but didn't cry out or move. "You really put him out, didn't you?" the guard asked with a short, hoarse laugh.

The man crouched over Ruff then, and Justice heard him say, "You dumb bastard. You poor, dumb bastard." Across his shoulder, the guard told the smith, "Some of 'em don't learn until it's too late. Well, he's Harry Hammerschmidt's meat now."

It was ten minutes before a second guard arrived. They threw a bucket of water on Ruff and he decided that was his cue to come around. He sat up, rubbing his face, staring blankly at the guards through his hair.

"Get up, Justice," they told him.

Ruff obliged. Supporting himself with the wall, he managed to stagger to his feet. Then each guard took an arm and they half-dragged him out into the harsh daylight of the yard.

Ruff was led past the knots of prisoners in the yard, stumbling and tripping as he went.

"Damn you!"

Ruff's eyes shifted to find Rackets, his face drawn miserably, his fists clenched, shouting at him. "Damn you, Ruff Justice!"

Ruff was being taken away, and with him went Rackets' chance of escaping. He couldn't forgive that.

The guards guided Ruff through a wooden gate in a stone wall. Two other guards stood watching expressionlessly. Through the gate they went into a narrow enclosed courtyard. One of the guards knocked on a door with his baton, and it opened to admit Ruff and his escort.

"Justice, Ruffin T.," he heard someone say. "Number 1574."

"Justice." This voice was cold yet oddly jubilant. It belonged to Harry H. A hand grabbed Ruff's hair, and his head was yanked up. Harry H. was staring at him, his eyes glittering. "I knew you'd end up my meat, hardcase." He was positively panting. There was something not quite right in Harry H.'s head. He placed his face close to Ruff's and said, "The years are going to go by, pal. Years. And you and me—we'll be together. You're not going to like it a bit."

As he spoke, Harry H. ground the heel of his boot down on Ruff's toe, and the pain he was able to produce with this simple torture was remarkable. Ruff fought back the impulse to smash his fist into Harry's face. That would serve no purpose now except getting himself beaten to death.

"Hardcase!" Harry H. laughed in contempt. "Show him his quarters, Luther," the assistant warden said. "Oh," he added as if he had forgotten some minor detail, "and do show Mr. Ruff Justice what sort of special services we provide here."

Luther, who looked Mexican but spoke unaccented English, promised to do that. Then he and Harry H. enjoyed a good laugh.

One moment Ruff was standing there watching the guards and the next he was being dragged down a dark stone corridor, his head throbbing, his guts turning over. He had a faint recollection of something hard striking him

32

behind the ear, of going down in a heap, but that was all vague and far away, as if it had happened to someone else.

The pain in his head was far from vague. He realized now that he had gotten himself into a tight situation. Harry H. was more than hard, he was a man who enjoyed hurting people. Maybe he enjoyed killing them. Maybe Mando Reyes was already dead . . . Christ, that would be a joke! Reyes dead and Ruff Justice locked in this dark tomb where he could never be found unless it suited Harry H.

They wound through progressively darker corridors. The guards had to duck because of the low ceilings. There was the stink of urine and sweat, of blood and of death in this hole.

Ruff was thrown into a cell which was stone-walled, no more than twelve by twelve. They weren't through with him yet.

The guard stepped in, kicked Ruff on the hip with a heavy, steel-toed boot which sent fiery pain through Ruff's leg. Then he laughed—damn the man, he laughed! Ruff got to his feet. That was a mistake. The guard moved in, clubbing at Ruff's head with a gloved hand which felt like leather-encased granite. His head was jarred from side to side as Ruff was backed up against the wall by the grinning guard.

Ruff felt for an angry, crimson moment like fighting back, like tearing the throat from this bloody bastard, but he controlled himself, knowing that he could achieve no more, that he could only lose in that way. A knee caught him in the groin and bile filled his throat, his head spun with sickness. The fist landed on his jaw again, and he went up on his toes. He had thought the smith could punch, but this—this was incredible. The man had pile drivers for arms. And where the smith had been fighting only out of anger, the guard enjoyed it. He relished every moment of it, slamming his fist into Ruff's nose, kicking out savagely at his knee.

Ruff tried the old trick—he went down and played possum.

That had stopped the smith, but it didn't even slow down the guard much. Savage kicks smashed into his ribs, hips, and then a boot toe caught his head and whatever else the guard might have done to him was lost in the heavy, pain-inspired fog which closed around Ruff, smothering his senses, blacking out the world.

4

IT WAS A hazy awakening. He was aware of the stone against his face, of the violent pain which seemed to throb through his entire body, of the thin shaft of yellow light which beamed saberlike through a high window.

He was aware of all of that, but it seemed to have no connection with him, with Ruff Justice. Justice was a high plains man, and he was definitely not on the plains. There was no wind flattening the long grass, no far-reaching blue sky above.

Where was Four Dove? Had he slept without her? One eye opened slowly. It would not open far. It was puffed and cut.

He could see little enough and could make but little sense of what he did see. He was not in the Crow camp, that much he knew. Fort Lincoln? No, not with these stone walls.

Ruff closed his eyes, racking his brain for the answers. But they would not come, and his body undermined his attempts. He was exhausted, his wounds taking their toll, and the nagging of his mind was ignored as he slid off into black, thoughtless sleep.

When he came around again he knew exactly where he was. The punishment barracks of the state prison at

Tucson, Arizona Territory. It took a while longer to recall why.

The shaft of light had slid all the way across the floor and was now creeping slowly up the gray stone wall. There were dark stains on the wall, and it didn't take a hell of a lot of imagination to realize what they were.

Ruff got to a sitting position, his head hanging. It was a long while before he attempted standing, even longer before he made it.

He staggered to the window, chinned himself, and looked out. He had a view of a barbed-wire fence and the prison yard beyond.

Once inside the prison you'll have to manage to get yourself into the punishment barracks.

"Success," Ruff muttered. His mouth felt funny, and it was a time before he realized he still had it padded with strips of rag. Now he removed them and tossed them out the window, hoping that it wasn't premature.

We don't know who we can trust inside the prison, so you'll have to take your chances. It could be a little mean.

Ruff's head came up. Two hulking forms stood in the doorway, and Ruff cowered away from them, backing into the corner. The fighting was over, he hoped. It served no further purpose; and the best way to keep them from beating him was to become suddenly submissive—he hoped.

"What's the matter, hardcase?" the Mexican asked. Ruff didn't like his smile a bit. He turned his face to the wall.

"Don't hit me," he begged.

"Don't hit him! Pretty tough hombre, isn't he, Ned?" Both men laughed. "I'm not going to hit you, Justice, Ruffin T. But you've bought it now. We've got some *really* tough men in here. You don't watch yourself, they'll eat you up."

He heard something metallic clatter against the floor,

but he didn't turn his head until they were gone. Then he walked stiffly to the plate of food they had left.

He ate on the hard, swing-down bunk, shoveling the food into his mouth with two fingers—you weren't allowed utensils in this barracks.

Then he sat, waiting until dark. It wasn't long in coming. There was a brief red-violet flash in the high window. Then the day dulled, the room settled to darkness. A small night creature scuttled across the floor. Ruff crept to the door.

He put an ear against it, hearing nothing. Reaching into his boot, he pulled out one of the roughly made keys. He fiddled with the lock for five minutes before hearing a satisfying click. Smiling thinly, he played with the lock again until the bolt slid to again.

I don't know how you're going to bust out of there. We'll try to get you some help. But it'll be dangerous, Ruff, you know that. If they catch you, they'll kill you. Of course, compared to what will come later, maybe the punishment barracks in a nice safe prison will be a bit of heaven.

Ruff sagged into the bunk and tried to sleep. And sleep he did, in fits and starts, when the pain allowed it. The old dreams came back again, and when they did he woke up suddenly in a cold sweat. After that he didn't try to sleep anymore.

At daylight the door slammed open and Harry H. stepped into the cell. The guard named Yates was with him. Neither of them looked as if they were going to invite Ruff to a tea party.

Yates closed the door behind him and leaned against it. Harry H. crossed the room, slapping his palm with a short, nasty-looking truncheon. Ruff backed away—trying his best to look panicked, broken. It wasn't all that difficult.

"You've made a nuisance out of yourself, Justice,"

37

Harry said. His eyes glittered under heavy eyebrows. "Since the minute you came through those gates. I didn't like you at first sight."

As he spoke he came nearer to Ruff, and Ruff backed away until he was pressed against the wall behind him. Uncomfortably, vividly, he recalled the bloodstains on that wall. Harry H. continued to slap the truncheon rhythmically against his palm.

"There's something wrong about you, Justice," Harry H. said. Justice's eyes, despite his efforts, must have flickered slightly at that. Harry H. nodded to himself.

"What do you mean?" Ruff said, putting a tremor in his voice.

"I don't know." Across his shoulder he said, "There's something wrong about him, isn't there, Yates? That's what I said from the first."

Yates nodded as if it was the least interesting thing he had ever heard. Ruff started to speak again but never got the chance. Harry's hand went up suddenly and then came down hard. A stunning pain went through Ruff's shoulder where Harry had struck him.

Ruff went to his knees, although the pain, bad as it was, wasn't enough to put him there. He peered up at Harry H. through the screen of his hair. Harry was smiling.

"Tough," he spat. "Real tough." His boot shot out and caught Ruff on the hip, almost on top of the bruise he already had there. The pain knifed through his leg.

"I don't like you, Justice," Harry said, bending low, panting as he spoke. "There's something that don't ring true. And I'll get it out of you. It might take months— that's all right with me. I've got the time. I'll come visiting every day. No regular time. Maybe in the middle of the night to sweeten up your dreams. But I'll be around."

Harry turned as if to go, thought better of it, and spun back, giving Ruff a parting shot with the truncheon. It was a perfect tap. He caught Ruff over the ear with it and Ruff went down—and this time he wasn't faking.

The floor beneath him started to tilt crazily, the walls to spin around him, and then Ruff fell off into a bottomless gray tunnel, Harry H.'s laughter echoing after him.

When he awoke it was daylight, and that didn't seem right. But he wasn't imagining the sunlight streaming through the high window. He watched the dust motes dance in the beam with great interest for a very long time.

There was a dull hammering behind his ears, and his stomach felt deflated, dry. Slowly Ruff got to his feet. He made it to the bunk before the nausea took over completely.

Ruff buried his face in his hands, fighting back anger—it would do no good at all to get angry. He felt like calling it off for a moment. Just get up and say, "Wire Major Harkness at Fort Thomas. He'll tell you who I am."

That feeling didn't last long. He had been sent here to do a job, and he couldn't ever recall having backed away from a job. Besides, he had a lot invested in this one. He would hate to think all of this had been for nothing.

But perhaps it was. He wasn't much nearer his goal than he had been the day he had started. *I'll be back.* He remembered Harry's words, and it produced an involuntary grimace. It was intimidating, he had to admit. A prisoner locked in these cells with no hope of getting out, ever. Harry was lord and master. He could see that you didn't eat, didn't sleep. How long could a man take it? Ruff Justice didn't intend to find out. He had to push it a little; the break would have to come soon.

At noon, or near then, Luther came in with a plate of food and a tin cup of water, and Ruff waited until he left to eat it. Then he lay on his bunk, going over his plan of escape. It stank—it all depended on optimism.

There was the door to the cell. That was no problem.

Then an outer door, and a wire fence, well guarded. The adobe wall came next, then the flats. The double-trenched outer fence—that was no problem if he made it that far, he thought. It was no good! He threw his hands up.

Harkness had said that there was someone inside who might be able to help. Ruff hoped to God the man showed up soon.

He lay back on his bed, watching the shifting shadows, listening to the distant voices of men in the yard beyond the window. At sundown Harry H. came and practiced his truncheon work, apparently just for the fun of it.

"It gets worse, Justice," the assistant warden said, stepping back, perspiring from his efforts. Ruff peered up at him through a swollen eye, holding his battered ribs. "I want to know who you are, what you're doing here. You smell to me, Justice. I never seen a man get in so much trouble so quick. That worries me, mister, indeed it does."

Then Harry turned and strode toward the door, leaving Yates to throw Ruff onto his bunk and close the door. "You get smart," Yates said in a hoarse whisper. "Tell Harry everything. There's worse places than this, Mr. Justice. You ain't even scratched the surface."

Then Yates was gone, the door slamming behind him. Yates' words lingered. *There's worse places than this. You ain't even scratched the surface.*

True? Probably—why else would Yates offer the warning? Ruff stood and paced the floor, turning Yates' words over in his mind, comparing them with those of Major Harkness.

He's no help to us. Mando Reyes is in the deepest darkest hole in that prison.

Then this would have to be carried a step further. Ruff grimaced at the thought. It would inevitably mean more beatings. Ruff felt like a drowning man being asked to let go of his last chance. He was being sucked deeper and deeper into the sublegal caverns of the prison. He wondered vaguely how Harry H. managed all of this. Didn't the warden know, or didn't Donovan care? And why, exactly, did Hammerschmidt go about things the way he did? Was it all sadism? Lord knows there seemed to be a wide enough streak of that in him, but there had to be more to it.

He stretched out on his bunk again, the very act of lying down to rest bringing sharp stabs of pain to his spine, hip, and back. His head continued to throb dully. That had been so constant that Ruff had almost grown accustomed to it.

He watched the ceiling, wondering. Wondering at Harry H., and Donovan, at the madman, Mando Reyes, and at one who seemed even madder, Ruff Justice, who had volunteered himself to be beaten and deprived and very probably killed.

He didn't have to wait long for the next step. Harry H., driven by some private impatience, returned at midnight. He stood silhouetted in the doorway, a silent second figure behind him.

Harry grunted to himself and moved in. Ruff watched him, listening to his breathing, to the whisper of boot leather against stone. He let Harry H. lift his truncheon, but that was as far as he let it go.

Ruff hurled himself from the bunk, lunging at Harry H.'s throat. The truncheon arced down, but Ruff was already inside of it. Harry's forearm slammed against Ruff's shoulder, but Ruff hardly felt it.

He had his hand around Harry's throat and he was pounding away with his other hand. He caught Harry flush on the jaw once and felt Harry's knees buckle.

Harry fought back wildly, bringing up a knee which glanced off Ruff's thigh, pounding clumsily at Ruff's back with his truncheon.

Yates was rushing toward them from the doorway, and Ruff knew it was only a matter of seconds before they overpowered him, but he made full use of his time. He slammed his fist into Harry H.'s face twice, hearing bone crack, feeling the hot rush of blood against his hand which still throttled Harry. Harry's eyes bulged and he clawed desperately at Ruff, trying to tear that hand free.

He gurgled oddly, and Ruff drove his free hand into Harry's soft gut. Suddenly Yates was all over him and the three of them went down in a heap.

For the next few moments it was a wild melee, hands and feet striking blows at random. Harry hit Justice and then Yates as he squirmed and writhed, Ruff's weight pinning him to the floor. Yates hit Harry H. as often as he hit Ruff, but after a minute or so they got organized.

Yates pinned Ruff's arms and Harry H. rolled from under the tall man. They pressed Ruff to the floor, Yates straddling him, and together they began a methodical beating.

Harry's fist piled into Ruff's head and torso. Harry must have lost his truncheon, but he hadn't lost his eagerness. He grunted with each blow as he threw it, and he muttered, "You bastard, you dirty bastard," as he worked.

Ruff tried to roll with the punches, but that was only marginally effective, pinned as he was.

"I'll kill you!" Harry shrieked suddenly. Yates muttered something and Harry H. told him to shut up.

"It's not worth it, Harry," Yates said. Hammerschmidt's blows stopped abruptly. Ruff, playing possum—he was getting good at it—heard Harry answer.

"No." He wiped back his hair. "No, it's not worth it. Not for this son of a bitch. I'm through with him, Yates! Through with him. Throw him in the hole."

"Harry!" Yates' voice was pleading.

"The hole, goddammit!"

"Sure, Harry. All right," Yates said, pacifying his boss. Ruff felt Harry's weight shift, felt the man get off his back. And moments later he felt the last, violent kick, which took him square on the liver, shooting stunning, fiery pain through Justice. And the pain brought anger. He wanted to come to his feet, to tear the throat out of the man, but he swallowed it and remained where he lay, face against the stone, his fists clenched, his heart racing.

He could hear Harry H.'s ragged breathing as he hovered over him for a long minute. Then Harry's voice, taut and distant, ordered Yates, "Get him out of here. Now!"

Harry stalked out of the room, and Yates stood there silently. Ruff opened an eye a fraction of an inch and saw Yates walk heavily to the door, lift an arm, and wait for a second guard.

Together then they picked Ruff up by his arms and dragged him out of the cell. They went around a corner and down a flight of rough stone steps, dropping Ruff once. Justice listened to the two men talking.

"The dumb bastard," Luther said. "He thought he was in hell. Jesus, that was paradise up there!" Luther chuckled at his own observation.

"Shut up," Yates growled.

"Sure. You're tough tonight, ain't you? Say—going into Tucson tomorrow? I'll go with you. I know a girl who's got a sister that won't quit."

"Open the door," Yates said.

Ruff heard a key turning in a heavy lock. He hoped it was as primitive a lock as the others in this prison. "Drag him in."

"Say, what does Harry think he's got here?" Luther asked. "I never heard of this man before."

"Harry knows. Harry smells it," Yates responded.

"Harry knows. Harry scares me sometimes."

"Harry's made you a wealthy man. What were you be-fore?" Yates demanded. "A low-life prison guard."

43

"Yeah, that's true. Still . . ." Luther's thoughts and voice trailed off. Ruff was being dragged along a floor which was of clay, straw-covered, rough. He opened his eyes a hair, seeing little by the light of the lantern Yates had picked up somewhere.

There was only the corridor, cut out of the earth, the scents of urine, of blood, of death, and the two men above him. Wherever they were taking him, Ruff Justice didn't want to go. He had a sudden notion to stand and take them on, but that was foolish. There were two of them and they had their guns.

Besides, he wasn't sure yet. Wasn't totally sure that this was where Reyes was being kept. He wasn't even sure that Reyes was alive. With Harry H., he decided, you never knew.

"Open up!" Yates' voice was a hiss. Ruff heard a door open, saw by the flickering lanternlight a wrinkled, hairless face, saw a door open.

Then they were through and Ruff was dropped. He felt hands lift his ankles, felt shackles being locked to them. Then he was dragged on.

They didn't go far. Twenty feet and he was thrown into a small hollow—it couldn't be called a cell. Dug out of the earth, it was no more than six feet high, perhaps twenty long. They were fifty feet below ground level, Ruff guessed, and after Yates and Luther turned away, it was totally dark. Dark and empty and cramped.

Black as a coal mine at midnight. Ruff backed away from the door, dragging his chains with him. He found a wall and placed his back against it, breathing heavily as his eyes struggled to penetrate the darkness, to see anything.

There was no such luck. The darkness was complete. The emptiness was not so complete. A hand touched Ruff's, and as Ruff jerked his hand away a mad cackling filled the cavern.

His head was near to Ruff's, and although he could see no features of that face, he knew. He knew that he had found his man. The mad and brutal savage, Mando Reyes.

5

THE HAND THAT clamped down on Ruff Justice's upper arm in the darkness was incredibly strong. He could hear breathing, not quite human, and smell the stink of a man long confined.

"Who are you?" the voice asked as the man scooted even nearer, never letting go of Ruff's arm. "I don't know you. I'll kill you."

"That won't help you get out of here, Mando," Ruff said evenly. The grip on his arm loosened. The breathing stopped and then resumed more slowly.

"Who are you?"

"Ruff Justice."

"I don't know you. How come you know my name?"

"They told me they were going to put me in with the toughest man in Arizona—that could only be Mando Reyes," Ruff lied calmly.

"Yes?" Reyes' voice balanced between disbelief and pleasure. His hand fell away. "What you mean about getting out of here? No one gets out, hombre."

"I do. I've got friends."

"Friends! They forget you once you're inside."

"Not mine," Ruff said.

"It can't be done," Reyes said. "Don't you think I've tried?"

"It can be done." Ruff fell silent as a man walked down the low corridor; they could see his lantern swinging from side to side. By that thin light Ruff got a glimpse of Mando Reyes.

He was huge across the shoulders and through the chest. His black hair was long and matted. A wild, curling beard grew out in all directions, hiding his mouth. Black eyes glittered.

"How?" Reyes hissed after the lantern had disappeared.

"It won't be easy," Ruff said. "There's no easy way."

"I'm going," Mando said. His hand found Ruff's shoulder and squeezed.

"That's right. I need two men to do it."

"And then I find Harry Hammerschmidt and I kill him," Mando promised.

"No you don't," Ruff said. "We're going out. The hell with Harry H. I won't risk getting caught just for the sake of revenge."

"You don't know Harry H."

"I know him," Ruff said with genuine bitterness.

"He beats me," Mando went on as if Ruff had said nothing. "Ever' day. That's Harry's way. He wants what you have, what you know."

"What do you mean?"

Mando drew away from Ruff, and Justice had the uneasy, illogical feeling that although he could not see Mando Reyes, the big man could see him and was now appraising him, studying his expression.

"Say a man pulls a job," the Mexican said finally. "He gets caught, see. But he figures—well, I'll pull ten years but when I get out at least I've still got the loot. They di'n' make me talk, di'n' get that from me."

Mando's breathing was labored. "No, they di'n' get it. The sheriff di'n' get it, the judge di'n' get it. But Harry H., he'll get it. He's got a lot of time to work. He don't

47

care about the law or nothin'. He'll kick your ass, boy, till you tell him maybe where the loot is. Maybe you die first. Harry, he just says, 'Tough luck, boy,' and he goes on to the next one, huh?"

"He tried it on me," Ruff said, inventing as he went along, "but I wouldn't tell him a damn thing. He said he'd put me in with you and you'd kill me for him. Then he'd have you here till the day you died."

"That's the bastard!" Mando said with virulence. "That's why I got to kill him."

"Another time. Not before we get out. It's not smart."

"You sayin' I'm not smart?"

"I'm saying we have to get out of here—nothing else matters to me."

Mando was thoughtfully silent. "Nothin' else matters to me either. Wha's your name?"

"Justice."

"Justice. We gonna be all right, Justice. We'll be great *amigos*, huh?" He slapped Ruff's shoulder and squeezed it.

All friendly. But there was an edge to that voice. An implied threat, and Ruff Justice knew suddenly that what they had said about Mando Reyes was true—the man was absolutely mad.

You watch yourself with Reyes, Justice. He's terrorized half the border. He's been convicted of or suspected of committing rape, arson, robbery, murder. He killed a man for not having tobacco on him when Reyes wanted a smoke—one of his own men. He's unpredictable, violent, and completely mad.

He was all of that, but he was also the key to this. Mando had been sitting silently in the darkness for long minutes. Now suddenly he asked: "When? When do we go out?"

"Tonight," Ruff said. There was no point in waiting. The plan, such as it was, would have to do. Why wait until Harry H. had worked him over a dozen more times, draining his strength still more? "It'll have to be tonight."

"All right." Mando laughed loudly. "Tonight. Then you tell me, Justice, how we going to do this, man! How we going to make it? You a crazy person, Justice."

In response Ruff crept closer to Mando across the straw-covered cell floor. Searching, he found the shackles around Mando's ankles.

"What the hell you doing?" Reyes demanded. Then he heard a small clicking sound and one of the irons fell away. "By God, you a smart fellow, Justice! We'll be all right!"

Ruff removed the other end of the shackle and then got to work on his own chains. One of the locks was stubborn, but with fifteen minutes of work he managed to get free of the irons.

"Where'd you get the keys?" Mando asked. He was rubbing his ankles in the darkness.

"I made 'em. These locks aren't much."

"Made 'em!" Reyes bellowed a laugh. "You pretty smart fellow, Justice." There was a pause. "I hope you not too smart for poor old Mando."

"It should be dark out by now," Ruff replied. "Wait until you've got the circulation back in your feet and we'll have at it."

Mando grunted. Even that seemed threatening.

"And no killing," Ruff added. "If they catch us and bring us back, I don't want to swing. There's always another day."

"Sure, Justice. No killing." The mockery dripped from his words of assurance.

"I mean it."

"Look, Justice," Mando said, scooting nearer. "Don't threaten, see? Don't tell Mando what to do—not ever."

"You want to go with me?" Ruff asked. "Shut your mouth, then."

49

Reyes didn't like that and Ruff could sense the anger, the coiled muscles, but Mando said meekly, "Sure, Justice. You the boss on this job."

Ruff made a satisfied noise as if he accepted Reyes' pledge, but he knew he was playing with fire with this man. He was big, unstable, and violent. And Ruff Justice needed him badly.

"We'll be great *amigos,* Mando. We'll get out and find some women. Maybe do a few jobs together, huh?"

"Sure, Justice," Reyes said blandly. "You bet. Soon as we get out."

Ruff waited in the darkness while the hours passed. It was already dark outside, but he wanted it to be later. Later when the guards, their senses dulled by the long hours of standing watch, were only looking forward to getting off, to going home to bed, when the early-rising moon would be ready to set.

All of this could only be done by guesswork. Time had no real meaning in the dark pit of the cells. Finally he decided it was time.

He tapped Reyes on the leg, not wanting to speak. Like a cat, Reyes got to his feet, and together they went to the cell door. Ruff again put his homemade keys to work, trying the big iron padlock.

He got it in thirty seconds. The hasp opened and Ruff chucked the lock. The door swung open on creaking hinges. Ruff hesitated, listening while Mando pressed against his back. Then, nodding to himself, he slipped through and was out into the earthen corridor, ducking low, feeling his way along the wall toward the next door, Mando at his heels, silent as a shadow.

They reached the door, seeing a patch of dim light through the tiny barred window. Ruff peered out. There was a guard seated on a wooden chair within fifteen feet of the door. He was dozing, but how deeply asleep was he?

Mando prodded Ruff's back with a finger. Angrily Ruff jabbed his own finger at the window. Mando peered through, his wildly bearded face shadowed weirdly by the lanternlight, his black eyes fierce, like coals burning in his eyesockets.

Ruff went to his knees and began working at the lock. This one was a bitch. He tried both ends of the first key and had no luck at all. Slipping the other key, the one with the round ends, from his boot, he tried again.

He was aware of the irony. The great escape might end right here. Mando and he would have no choice but to go back to the cell, and lock themselves in. If that happened, Mando Reyes would probably cheerfully strangle Ruff Justice.

The tumblers fell.

Ruff stood, feeling the sweat in his eyes. The guard had not heard the faint sound; he had not moved.

Ruff tried the door, and almost with surprise he felt it open an inch or two. He glanced at Mando, whose jaw was hanging open with animal ferocity. He passed a finger in front of his throat and then shook his head negatively. Mando looked disappointed, but he nodded agreement— the guard would not be killed.

Ruff opened the door a foot, his heart pounding. Now he could see the guard's chest rising and falling gently, see the pistol which was holstered on his hip. Ruff darted through the door and across the small room, his fist lifting to come down with all of his strength behind the guard's ear.

Soundlessly the man slumped to the floor. Ruff bent to lift the pistol and met Mando's hand. Their eyes locked. Mando's hand was already closed around the butt of the Colt. Slowly Ruff stood, shrugging. Mando tucked the pistol into his waistband.

Ruff went to the next door. This one was simple, and he opened it in seconds.

Together they slipped down a long stone corridor, their boots whispering against the floor. The outer door was all that remained. Was there a guard or not? Ruff couldn't recall.

There wasn't. He slipped the lock and then they were through, out into the warm desert night. The shadows of the prison building were long. The moon was sinking toward the horizon. A few sheer clouds drifted across the sky, screening the stars. They could see the guards at the watchtowers.

Mando had hold of Ruff's sleeve, like a child not wanting to get separated. Ruff shook him off. They moved ahead to the gate which led from the punishment barracks area into the exercise yard. Ruff worked at the lock until the sweat drenched his body, without success. It couldn't all be frosting.

"We've got to go over," Ruff whispered, pulling Mando's head close to his mouth, pointing a finger up.

Mando nodded. The gate was set in a wooden frame, topped with barbed wire. But there was a gap between the wall of the storehouse next door and the beginning of the wire. It wasn't much of a gap, but it would do.

Ruff boosted Mando, and the big man, agile and quick, caught the top of the wall and drew himself up. A big hand dangled toward Ruff, and he caught it, feeling himself pulled up. They wriggled over, dropping to the ground on the far side, the barbed wire tearing Ruff's sleeve.

Staying close to the buildings on their right, they moved toward the outer wall. Their shadows were concealed by the awnings of the buildings, and they made it easily to the end of the block buildings.

Now there was fifty feet of open ground to the twenty-foot-high adobe wall. Ruff glanced at Mando Reyes. The big man was practically slavering. His fist was tight around the butt of that Colt he carried. He was mad enough to touch off a shot at the guards above them along the watchtower. Ruff placed a hand on his wrist, and the big man calmed slightly.

There was no way across the yard except guts and luck. Ruff took a deep breath. They watched the routine of the guards in the watchtower for nearly half an hour, knowing that every minute they delayed there was an increased chance that the turnkey in the punishment block would come to and sound the alarm.

It had to be done. Ruff waited until the guard turned away. Then, sucking it up, he dashed for the wall. Fifty feet—a man could cover it quickly, but it seemed to be miles. Ruff expected a shout of alarm, a bullet at any moment. But it didn't come.

He stood against the outer wall, chest rising and falling, watching Mando Reyes. Suddenly Mando started to run. It was an ungainly, loping run, but he covered ground with it, and in another second Mando was beside him, grinning as he pulled deep breaths into his massive chest.

So much for the easy part. Now to get over the main wall, across the flats, and through the wire. The entire scheme seemed suddenly crazy to Ruff Justice. Maybe, he thought, I am mad, as mad as Mando Reyes.

Going over the massive wall was not possible. It could not be climbed, and it was topped with barbed wire. There was no way a guard could miss the activity anyway. There were several smaller service gates along the wall, Ruff knew, but they were just under the towers, directly in the guards' line of sight.

Nevertheless, it was the only way.

They flitted through the shadows, two desperate men, expecting a bullet at any moment. Ruff eased along, his back scraping the wall, Reyes in his tracks.

Ruff halted suddenly. He had seen movement in the shadows. The figure of a man. Reyes had drawn his pistol, and he gripped Ruff's shirt questioningly.

Ruff moved on slowly, puzzled. He had only seen the man for a moment, but in the almost pitch blackness, it had looked for all the world like ...

Mando tugged his shirt again, and Ruff halted. The small gate was before them. Ruff went to it, fishing for his keys. He didn't need them—the gate stood open an inch or two. Mando was on his heels, and he decided to play with the lock for a moment anyway. The last thing he needed was for Mando's suspicions to be fed by something like this.

He wasted a few minutes on the lock and then swung the gate open another foot. Nodding his head, Ruff Justice crept through, wondering how Major Harkness had gotten to Warden Donovan. For it had been the warden in the shadows, Ruff was sure of it. It had been the warden who had left the gate open.

The moon was sinking in the west. Slowly the land went dark. Thin starlight cast dim shadows across the flats from the bases of the low growing brush. They clung to the wall until the moon was completely gone, until the night had gone dark and silent, and then they crept out onto the flats, not daring to breathe or look back at the guards in the watchtowers.

Breathlessly they ran on, and Ruff began to worry about the dogs. He knew there were dogs, and they should have already been baying, barking, rushing after them. But the night was silent.

He could see nothing. The fence ahead of them was still far distant, but the guns had not yet opened up, and Ruff began to believe, to hope, that they might make it.

Suddenly the fence was in sight. A low, tangled web of wire pasted to crooked posts, bordered by those trenches. It rose against the sky like a black, menacing web, and Ruff felt his gut tighten. They might make it—might—but after that was another fifty miles of desert, and they would be afoot; the plan itself was insane, the men who followed it madmen.

And then they were there. No roar of guns had split the silence. There was only the ragged breathing of the two men. No dogs. That bothered Ruff. No dogs, when he knew there were supposed to be dogs. The only explanation, of course, was that the warden had kept them in.

"How now?" Mando gasped. Ruff showed him.

He took a running start and with arms flailing, leaped the trench, landing in a heap next to the web of barbed wire. He could see Mando across the ditch, see the Mexican back up and with a wild, running start, hurtle over the trench.

"Come on!" Ruff's whisper was low and urgent. He walked and then ran along the fence, searching for that extraordinarily crooked post. Finding it, he got to hands and knees and searched for and found the wire clippers.

"Bueno," Mando said. His teeth flashed briefly in the starlight. Ruff Justice turned away and began snipping the wire. The sounds were crisp, metallic in the night.

It took ten minutes but finally they were through the coils of wire, although Ruff had had his arm and cheek torn open by the jagged barbs of the fence wire.

"Now what?" Mando asked. His breathing was shallow.

"Wait."

"That ditch, it's twelve feet deep."

Ruff was busy clipping wire from the fence. Mando was incensed.

"What are you doing, Justice?"

"Getting us out of here," Ruff answered angrily.

"You not doing it damn fast!"

His voice rose. It could have been audible for half a mile.

"Shut up," Justice muttered. Mando Reyes pulled that Colt he was carrying, and Ruff coiled to leap at him, but slowly, sullenly, Mando put it away.

"Let's go," Ruff said. They had only to clear the second trench. It was nearly twelve feet deep, too wide to jump. Ruff, holding a length of wire overhead, slid into the ditch. Mando followed in a cloud of dust. The big man jolted hard against the bottom of the trench.

"Now what?" Reyes asked.

"Up."

"It's twelve feet."

Ruff nodded impatiently. Suddenly the man wanted everything explained as if they had all the time in the world.

"How tall are we?" Ruff asked. Mando looked at him crookedly. "Brace yourself," Justice told him. "I'm going up."

Reyes stood against the side of the trench, and Ruff clambered up. By placing his feet on Reyes' shoulders he was just high enough to get a grip on the edge of the ditch.

Ruff chinned himself, one hand slipping momentarily. Then he managed to throw a leg up and rolled free. He crouched, panting, beside the ditch.

"Now what?" Mando hissed.

"Now you," Ruff replied. "But first throw up that pistol."

"What d'you mean?"

"Throw me that gun. I want it."

"Go to hell, Justice!"

"All right." Ruff shrugged. "So long, Mando."

"Wait!" the big man shouted as Ruff started to rise and turn away. "You want the damn pistol, you take it."

He lobbed it up and Ruff caught it, tucking it away in the waistband of his pants. Then, uncoiling the barbed wire he had cut, he wrapped it around his wrist, tossing the other end to Mando.

"Watch yourself," Ruff warned him. Mando only grumbled a response. But he took the wire firmly and began to climb. Within moments he too was up and over. He rolled to a sitting position, sucking at his hand.

"Come on," Ruff said.

"You go yourself, Justice. Me, I'm going it alone."

"You've got a better chance with me." Ruff smiled. "I've got the gun."

"Yeah." Mando's voice was a low growl.

Together they began to run across the desert. Mando went down twice, Ruff once, over unseen obstacles. Ruff's own breathing was loud in his ears. The footing was sandy, the night warm. But they couldn't have long. They just couldn't.

He swiveled his head back across his shoulder frequently, watching for the pursuit that was bound to come. Abruptly he stopped.

"What was that?" Reyes had heard it too. He was crouching, looking at Ruff expectantly.

Horses. Nickering. And not far distant. Reyes got to his feet and automatically turned away from the sound, which seemed to originate in a clump of willow near the dry wash they now traveled.

"Wait." Ruff turned the other way, toward the horses, and Reyes, muttering a beautiful Spanish oath, followed.

The horses stood in the willows, tethered loosely. They had a bale of hay scattered about the ground. They had been there for some time, all day, maybe longer. Their saddles rested on the ground nearby.

"What is . . ." Mando hesitated, fearing a trap. Ruff was already throwing a saddle over the stocky buckskin. There was a full half-gallon canteen on the pommel, and in the saddlebags were tins of food.

"Get with it, Mando."

"How did this get here? Whose horses are these?"

"They're ours," Ruff said, trying to sound as if he himself had expected it all along. "Friends of mine left them for me."

Mando saddled quickly, but his face was dubious as Ruff glanced at it in the starlight. Justice was sitting the buckskin, watching Reyes cinch his saddle, when the sounds of dogs first echoed across the flats.

"They're on to us," Mando said angrily. He swung into the saddle.

"Where to now?" Ruff asked.

"The border, *cabrón*—where else?" Mando asked. He kneed his pony forward, heading due south, and Ruff Justice, suppressing a satisfied smile, followed.

6

•••• ⎯⎯⎯◈⎯⎯⎯ ••••

THE LAND WAS a raw, empty thing. The desert wind
lifted the light sand and hurled it at their faces. The
horses lowered their heads and plodded on beneath the
fierce sun.

They saw nothing either behind or ahead. Nothing but
red rock, cracked white playas, and the occasional clumps
of brittle gray-green brush.

If there was pursuit back there, they were far, far behind. The sun hammered down, and Ruff felt the sweat
trickle from his body, felt the furnacelike wind dry it.

They were into an area of white sand now, and Ruff
squinted against the blinding glare, following the silent
Mando Reyes southward, ever southward.

A low line of mountains, black against the overpowering white of the sands, began to appear to their right.
Nothing grew there. To their left a sea of dunes rose, running away endlessly to the east.

Mando held up a hand, and Ruff saw him swing
down. He had found a scrawny, lacelike mesquite bush
and sat in the shade, not watching Ruff's approach.

Justice dismounted as well, removing his saddle. The
buckskin munched unhappily on the mesquite beans
which were scattered about.

"Too damn hot," Mando said. That was more than he

had said all morning. Ruff wanted to talk to him, to draw him out, but it seemed safer to maintain his own silence.

He watched the horse chew mesquite beans, its snuffling nostrils blowing sand as it lowered its head. A stream of giant red ants ran in a wavering line from the mesquite to an indefinite, distant point. A lone vulture circled high in a clear, superheated sky.

They rested in the meager shade through the heart of the day. Mando slept, but although Ruff's eyelids were heavy, he didn't give in to the temptation to siesta. You never knew with Mando Reyes.

Ruff sat apart, the gun tucked into his waistband, and once he saw Mando's eyes open slightly, saw the black eyes measure him. Justice himself munched on some of the bitter mesquite beans. He knew the Indians in this area used them for a sort of bread, but they were nearly unpalatable unprepared, although the horses didn't seem to think so.

"How far's the border, Reyes?" Ruff asked, knowing the big man was not asleep.

"Maybe ten miles," he said from out of the nest of tangled black beard.

"They'll never catch us," Ruff commented. Mando's answer was a grunt. Not once had Mando thanked Ruff for getting him out of the prison. His gratitude was as likely to be shown with a bullet in the end, if he was given half a chance.

Reyes didn't like Ruff. It was obvious. Of course maybe Reyes didn't like anyone.

As the sun dropped lower they saddled again and rode on, angling nearer to the mountains. Now, in the shadow of the mountains, ocotillo with crimson tips and low-growing, silvery cholla cactus flourished. Once in the high reaches of the stark, denuded hills Ruff caught sight of a single wind-tortured cedar.

They still had water, but not for long. Ruff drank a

mouthful, tepid, tasteless, from his canteen and settled into the saddle. Ten miles. And then what? What was Mando's plan after reaching the border?

When they had worked this out—Ruff, Major Harkness, and the marshal, Reeves—they had agreed that there was only one logical course for Mando to pursue. The trouble was, Mando was not a logical man.

The shadows were stretching out across the desert. The gullies were pools of black. Mando had crested a little ridge, with Ruff behind him, and now the big man pulled up. His arm lifted, and Ruff heard him give a grunt of satisfaction.

"There. You know what that is?"

Ruff squinted into the distances. A small, dirty collection of adobes squatted low in a dry valley.

"No."

"Del Cerro, hombre," Mando said with irritation. "That's Mexico, man. Come on."

The little town took on form as they approached it in the twilight, but it didn't get any more attractive. A pack of assorted dogs lay in the middle of the dusty main street—the only street. They rose to bark and circle the horses. Mando kicked out, catching one of the excited, leaping dogs in the chest with his boot. It ran away, whimpering, and the others followed.

"I know some people here," Mando said. "We get ourselves fixed up, huh?"

"Sure." Ruff nodded.

Mando swung down in front of the largest adobe. It had no sign, but by the noise, the smells, it was the cantina. Mando looped his horse's reins over the hitchrail and tramped inside, Ruff following.

Reyes stood there in the doorway, a big black-bearded man in torn and dusty prison garb, and the saloon fell silent. Faces turned slowly. Then one thin, pockmarked man heavy with guns rose to his feet.

"Mando!" Arms extended, he walked to Reyes. The bandit ignored the proffered hand, grunted the man's name, which was Chivo, and without asking, lifted one of Chivo's pistols, spun the cylinder, and tucked it behind his belt.

Ruff frowned. The two men muttered together, Mando flagging a thumb at Ruff Justice, Chivo, his dark eyes narrowed, nodding agreement to something.

Mando put a hand on the thin man's shoulder, then he turned and waved Ruff to him. Together they walked through the silent cantina to a back table. Ruff put his back to the wall and sat down.

The cantina gradually came to life again. A musician in a tight black suit strummed a guitar as he strolled among the customers. The conversation around them rose to a normal, loud pitch.

But they were not forgotten. Eyes flickered to the big, infamous bandit and his tall gringo companion. Both of them still dressed in prison clothes.

"We are safe here, Ruff Justice," Mando said. He actually patted Ruff's hand with his own scarred meathook. "We are among friends!"

Among Mando's friends anyway, Ruff reflected. Food was brought to them, and Mando bolted down three tamales and a platterfull of rice and beans, spooning the frijoles up with broken tortillas.

He had a beer and then a second and then another, and finally Mando settled back, patting his belly contentedly. He waited until Ruff was finished and then nodded his head. "Come on, we get us some clothes, huh?"

Mando led the way through a back door into a small office where Chivo waited. The thin man sat, arms folded, on the edge of a battered desk, smoking a cigar. Mando took the cigar from his lips, clamped it into his teeth, and began undressing. Chivo didn't utter a complaint.

The clothes they had been given were not much, but

they were clean. Jeans and peasant shirts—oversized, white, baggy. Ruff didn't tuck his in. He took the big sombrero from Chivo, nodded a *gracias,* and watched as Mando, before a chip of mirror, positioned his hat.

"I got to get rid of this," Mando said to Ruff. He rubbed the massive beard and yanked at his own hair. "I think I frighten away the children and the women—and I don' want to frighten away the women, Ruff Justice!" He barked a laugh and slapped Ruff on the shoulder.

"Why don' you take care of the horses, Ruff Justice?" he asked, cocking his head to one side, smiling enough to show a line of white teeth behind the mat of beard. "I think we have a long ride ahead of us, and we better take good care of those animals."

He said something in rapid Spanish to Chivo, and the thin man told Ruff in painfully wrought English, "The stable she at the end of the street." He pointed.

Ruff went out a back door Chivo showed him, into a stinking alley. The stars were bright and clear, the air still warm. A coyote howled in the distant foothills, and a town dog answered the primitive summons.

Ruff walked to the front of the cantina, watching the shadows move behind the lighted windows, listening to the furious strumming of the guitar. He untied the horses and led them to the end of the street, finding the stable, no more than a lean-to housing three mules and a pale horse.

There was no one around, and so Ruff unsaddled the horses and led them to water. Finished, he took them back to the lean-to and began rubbing them down with a piece of old sacking.

The hay was stacked in the corner. It was poor stuff, green and moldy, but the horses didn't mind.

Ruff Justice watched them eat for a moment, then he walked out into the stableyard, watching the moon rise. It was just above the dark, flat horizon, an orange, lopsided ball peering with surprise at the landscape. An owl dipped low and crossed the face of the moon. Then feet pounded up behind him, and Ruff Justice whirled, his hand dropping toward his gun.

He never got it up. The first man piled into him, his shoulder colliding with Ruff's ribs, and they went down in a heap.

Ruff grabbed his hair on the way down and yanked the man's face into his fist. Blood cascaded over both of them, and the man yowled. A boot landed on Ruff's ribs and he rolled aside, trying to sweep this attacker's feet from under him.

By now the first man was on his feet again, and as Ruff turned to meet him he saw starlight glinting on a knife blade.

The man lunged, and Ruff took him by the wrist and elbow, turning the knife arm inside out, bending the hand back until the knife dropped free. He lifted a knee hard into the man's groin, and he dropped to his face, clutching himself and moaning.

There were others now. Two more from out of the night, and Ruff saw a club arc downward. He shifted his head, but the club caught him a stunning blow on the shoulder. A man from in front of him leaped at Justice and clamped his hands around Ruff's throat. Ruff put his thumbs in the hollows beneath his attacker's ears and applied the pressure. It didn't take much of that for the thug to decide he wanted no more of Justice.

Ruff felt a boot slam into the back of his knee, felt that leg buckle, and he staggered and then went down in a heap.

He managed to chop a short, powerful right into the face of the first man on top of him, but after that it was all over. There were too many of them, and maybe they weren't good at their work, but they were enthusiastic.

Fists clubbed Ruff's head, and a solid, metallic something banged off his skull. It didn't put him out, but it knocked the fight out of him. His feet and arms no longer responded. He had to lie there and take it as they kicked him methodically. After a time he felt the pain no more.

Looking up, could see the men above him. Black, faceless figures against the starry sky. They were dragging him.

He must have gone out then, because when he was next aware of anything, it was of being tied hand and foot. The moon was riding high now, nearly white, staring down mockingly into a small enclosure where Ruff was being kept.

He struggled with the ropes for a minute and then heard a growled warning. There was a man with a gun standing just outside the enclosure.

He managed to sleep, or perhaps he blacked out again. Awakening, he found the yellow sun in his eyes. It was still low, the air cool. Long shadows painted the earth.

A Mexican with a torn, floppy sombrero crouched nearby, rifle across his knees.

"What's going on, hombre?" Ruff asked. "Why are you keeping me here?"

There was no answer. Maybe Mando Reyes had enemies in this town. Maybe the Mexicans figured there would be a reward for the two escaped convicts. Or this could be Mando's doings. Why? Ruff struggled to sit up. He looked at the white chickens scratching in the dust nearby, at the crooked, surrounding poles which made up the enclosure, where, by the smell, pigs were kept.

"Why do you have me tied up?"

Still no answer. The sun rose higher, the pen grew hotter. The chickens scratched on, making warbling clucking sounds.

A shadow fell across Ruff Justice, and he looked up to see Chivo standing there. The little man was grinning, exposing all of his overlong upper teeth.

"*Buenos dias,* Señor Justice."

"Where's Mando?"

Chivo shrugged. "He be along."

Then it was Mando's doing. Why? There could only be one reason, unless somehow Mando had tumbled to the game, which seemed very unlikely. There was only one sensible reason—Mando Reyes was through with Ruff. Now he would discard him.

"What's happening, Chivo? Why'd he do this to me?"

"Oh," Chivo shrugged, "he say he don't like you much, Justice. So he thinks he kill you." Chivo was still smiling. It didn't take much to amuse him.

"Listen . . ." Ruff's lowered voice was frantic. "I don't want to die, Chivo."

"No one does. We all do," Chivo said, shrugging yet again.

"Let me go." Ruff looked around. No sign of Mando yet. "Let me go and I'll make it worth it."

"Worth it? What have you got, Justice? To be worth it when Mando Reyes turns me inside out, huh?"

"I'll show you."

Chivo lifted an eyebrow, vaguely interested. Ruff sat with his ankles tied, his hands bound before him. "Let me have your knife, Chivo."

"What for?"

"Just let me have the knife," Ruff said impatiently.

Chivo, keeping his rifle ready, unsheathed his knife and tossed it to Ruff. It stuck in the ground, a hair too close to Ruff's groin to be funny. Ruff took the knife, his hands still tied, and as Chivo watched curiously he began prying at his bootheel. When the heel fell free, Ruff tossed the knife aside and his fingers removed something from inside the hollow heel.

It was wrapped in linen, and before Chivo's glittering eyes, Ruff uncovered it. It sparked in the sun like cold fire, a beautiful and ancient emerald ring set in yellow gold.

"*Madre de Dios*," Chivo whispered. He came forward, tossing the other guard his rifle. He took the ring from Ruff's fingers and held it up, examining it. "This is worth much."

"It's worth a fortune," Ruff told him. "And it's yours if you let me go."

Chivo's eyes came up from the ring. He told Ruff, "It's mine anyway, Mr. Justice." And then he laughed. A dry, shrill laugh which shook his shoulders. The light in his eyes changed, and the laugh broke off abruptly. Ruff knew exactly what was going on in Chivo's dark little mind.

When Mando showed up, Ruff was going to be killed. Why not kill him now before Mando saw the ring and claimed it, before Ruff could barter with Mando himself?

"Give me my rifle, Martinez."

The rifle was tossed through the air, and Chivo caught it deftly. Ruff found himself looking down the unblinking, black eye of a .44-40 Winchester. Chivo had already started to take the rifle to his shoulder when the sound of footsteps caused his head to come around.

Mando Reyes stood there, minus the beard but wearing a huge mustache. His eyes were flinty. Chivo sheepishly lowered the rifle.

He tried to pocket the ring he had in his hand, but Mando Reyes didn't miss much. His eyes flickered from Chivo to Ruff, noticing the knife and bootheel, and back to Chivo.

"What do you have, Chivo?"

Chivo whimpered a little laugh. "Nothing, Mando!" He grinned. Mando wasn't smiling in return.

"Give it to me."

Chivo hesitated a moment, then shrugged and, laughing again, he tossed it to Mando Reyes.

67

"You were going to keep this?"

"No, Mando."

"To keep it and kill Justice?"

"No, Mando. On my mother's soul."

Mando was a big cat when he moved. He was to Chivo in three steps, and a big fist clubbed Chivo down. Mando stood over him, panting. He kicked Chivo's rifle aside and kicked him viciously in the head, splitting open his face.

"Bastard," Mando muttered. "Lie to Mando Reyes! I ought to tear your throat out." His eyes were animal, his jaw worked spasmodically, and Ruff Justice saw the madness of Mando Reyes.

Justice thought he was going to kill Chivo, there could be no doubt about it, and then suddenly the man calmed. He smiled, bent over, and patted Chivo.

"Get up, Chivo, go have someone wash your face. Drink tequila, huh?"

Chivo, standing slowly, swaying on his feet, answered through broken teeth, "Sure, Mando, sure."

Then he turned and walked away, leaving his rifle on the ground. "You too, Martinez," Mando growled, and the other guard took off at a run. No fool that one.

Mando turned his attention to Justice. He crouched low, his broad dark face expressionless. The ring glittered in his hand.

"This is very old, hombre."

"Yeah."

"Where would a man find such an old ring? Obviously very expensive ring?"

"Look, Mando, you can have it. Just let me get out of here."

"I ask you a question, Justice!"

"I don't recall," Ruff answered. Mando's big fist shot out and caught Ruff flush on the jaw. His head reeling, Ruff hit the ground.

"You see, I think I have seen something like this before." Mando went on conversationally. Ruff's face was in the dirt, blood leaking from a cut on the cheek. "Very fine craftsmanship. Inside—you see—initials. A.M.F. Yes, this is very valuable. I ask you, Justice, where did you get it?"

"I don't know. Maybe in a card game—"

The fist shot out once again as Ruff tried to rise and slapped him backward. Mando's voice was deep and calm.

"Your secret does you no good dead."

"Mando!" Ruff got to a seated position again. His head hung and his voice was weary. "I found it long ago. Far north of here. It's impossible to go back."

"Indios?"

"Yes. Utes, and a savage lot of them."

Mando nodded. "Then I think—Colorado, no?"

"Colorado," Ruff agreed with a heavy, heavy nod.

Mando grinned. He was hunkered down before Ruff. His hand went to the back of his belt, and a knife appeared. He slit Ruff's bonds, first freeing the ankles and then the wrists.

"Now we are *amigos* again, huh?" Mando asked. He stretched out a big paw and rubbed Ruff's head.

"Sure. You're letting me go?"

"Let you go?" Mando grinned. "No, hombre. I cannot let you go." Mando stood and pulled Ruff to his feet. The tall man stood there rubbing his chafed wrists.

"Why not?"

"The ring, Justice. How can I let you go?"

"I told you all I know about it."

"But not enough. Come, let's talk some more." He threw a bearlike arm around Ruff's shoulders. "Let's have some food, some coffee, huh? We're *amigos* again, Ruff Justice. Great friends."

7

———◆———

Once Reyes gets a look at that ring—assuming you sur-
vive that long—we should have it made. I don't see how
anything can go wrong from then on.

Hoping Major Harkness was right, Ruff Justice rode
steadily southward, following the broad back of Mando
Reyes. They were well into Mexico now, following a
pretty little thread of a stream which glinted silver in the
sunlight and which stained the earth near it green in its
passing. There were willows and here and there a cotton-
wood along the creek. Twenty feet to either side of the
stream, however, the desert took over. The land was raw
and red and wild. A hulking red mesa was thrust up from
the earth to their right. Jumbles of volcanic stone—red
and glassy black—appeared at intervals, and they had to
detour around these lava fields or cut the horses' hoofs to
ribbons.

Almost over . . . almost over. Everything, difficult as it
had been, working to perfection. Why then did he have
this uneasy feeling which prickled the hairs on the back of
his neck and settled in his stomach like a stone?

"I think five miles," Mando said, slowing his horse to
allow Justice to come even with him.

"Five miles to where?" Ruff asked, although he already
knew.

"You'll see," Mando answered. "But tonight we shall dine and drink, and dance! You shall see, you shall see."

Mando started whistling and then singing, waving a hand in the air. That lasted for all of half a minute. Reyes suddenly stopped. His arm slowly fell and he hunched his shoulders, his face going sullen, his eyes glassy.

The man does have his spells, Ruff thought. Something was not quite right in that head—some little connection was not being made. Mando would shout and sing and then turn into a brooding, dark-eyed beast for no apparent reason. At those moments he was dangerous, deadly. Ruff slowed his horse just a little, wishing again that he had a gun. He had never thought he was the sort of man who needed one, needed to feel that hard reassuring weight to give him confidence. But with a man like Mando Reyes around it was a damn fine idea.

They didn't arrive at the rancho until dusk. The low grassy hills surrounding the big white house were flooded with purple light from the dying sun. The stream they had been following had broadened at this point, and there were wide meadows where hundreds of silky horses grazed.

It was all regal and quite beautiful. The low hills, the cottonwoods along the creek, the house itself with its red tile roof standing like a monument to opulence behind a high white wall.

"You know whose place that is, Mr. Justice?" Mando asked.

"No idea," Ruff replied.

"If I told you you'd fall off your horse."

"Are you going to tell me?"

"Not now. You'll see. When we get down there you will find out. Let me surprise you, eh?"

It wouldn't be much of a surprise. Mando led the way down into the valley, Ruff on his heels.

He'll bee-line it back to his boss. In his way Reyes is

loyal. Ernesto Valenzuela. I know you've heard the name. It's Valenzuela we want. The man's a butcher without conscience. He posed as a freedom fighter, a patriotic revolutionary, then slaughtered those foolish enough to follow him. He came across the border in '75—I guess you recall all that. He left a path of destruction, rape, and murder across New Mexico Territory. I don't know if you know this, Justice, but my wife and my two little boys were three of his victims.

Ruff could still vividly recall the set of Major Harkness's jaw, the steel in his eye when he reached that point.

The government wants Valenzuela, Ruff. But I want him more. Watch yourself. He's got an army down there with him.

Some of that army was starting to appear out of the shadows now. There was infantry near the great white wall surrounding Valenzuela's house, and off to the east, toward the river, cavalry was drifting in.

"It's me, Mando Reyes!" the big man called out loudly. He held both hands high in the air. "Mando! Hey, is that you, Ignacio? It's me, Mando, back from hell!"

They swung down from their horses before a huge and intricate iron gate. Dark-eyed soldiers wearing mustaches and crossed bandoliers came forward, their gaze shifting from Mando to Ruff and back again.

One of their leaders, the man Mando had called Ignacio, stepped forward and shook Mando's hand. They chatted together in Spanish, and the faces around Ruff relaxed a little. Still they looked him over warily. He tried to look innocuous.

"Come on," Mando said, and his voice was more of a command now than an invitation. "We go in."

They passed through the high, ornate iron gate and walked through the formal gardens planted before the imposing white house of Ernesto Valenzuela.

72

Up three steps they went under the huge portico and waited while Ignacio went in through the carved oak doors. They weren't left alone. Two men with rifles and deep scowls stood by, watching. Ruff was beginning to wonder just how welcome Mando Reyes was here. He recalled something the bandit had said about his friends: "Friends! They forget you once you're inside."

Maybe there was a reason for forgetting Mando Reyes. A man so obviously unstable might make an unreliable ally.

Ignacio was back. He nodded his head, inviting them in. Ruff noticed that Ignacio let Mando and himself precede him.

The ceiling of the house was high, heavily beamed. The carpet under foot was wine-red. Gilt-framed paintings hung on the white walls. The furniture was massive and dark in the Spanish style.

They were led into a huge, lavishly decorated room, perhaps a ballroom at other times. A suit of armor stood in one corner, on the wall before Ruff an ancient shield with antique swords projecting from it spokelike. There was a heavy desk and a liquor cabinet nearly twenty feet long, well stocked. The room was dark, cool, and luxurious.

There was a man behind the desk. He wore a white silk shirt, a sardonic smile, a thin mustache over a narrow, cruel mouth. Ernesto Valenzuela himself. The house, the man, all were as Ruff had expected, as they had been described to him in that extensive briefing.

No one had described the tall woman who stood behind Valenzuela, and that was unforgivable. She was well worth describing.

Tall, sleek, full-breasted, with haughty dark eyes and full, curving lips, she was beautiful, incredibly so, in the Spanish mold. Olive complexion, erect carriage, hair drawn tightly back and decorated with a high comb. Her black eyes flitted across Ruff Justice, seeming to register brief amusement.

There was nothing like amusement in the eyes of Ernesto Valenzuela. He looked from Mando to Justice and back.

"This is a happy surprise, Mando," Valenzuela said. He didn't look surprised or happy to Ruff. "And who is this you've brought to us?"

"His name is Ruff Justice, Señor Valenzuela. He—"

"Mr. Justice," Valenzuela interrupted. His manner was suave. "I am Ernesto Valenzuela. Welcome to my home. My wife, Soledad," he said, introducing the woman. Ruff nodded formally. The woman's eyes flashed again.

"We must have wine." Valenzuela lifted a finger, and a white-coated servant appeared from nowhere.

"Not for me, *gracias*," Ruff said.

"No?" Valenzuela looked vaguely irritated.

"I do not have a taste for wine, Señor Valenzuela. I do not drink."

"Mando?" Valenzuela asked. "You have not lost the taste for drink? Wine?"

"*Por favor*, Señor Valenzuela." Mando held his hat in his hands, looking like a peasant supplicant before the great landowner. But there was a cold light in the murky depths of the bandit's eyes, and Ruff wondered how it would be if Valenzuela were not surrounded by his army.

The servant silently poured wine from a crystal decanter into silver goblets. Valenzuela looked meditatively into his goblet and then, turning to his wife, dismissed her with a few short words.

"Gentlemen," Valenzuela said with a quickly fading smile, "sit down."

Mando had no sooner seated himself than Valenzuela, leaning forward, demanded, "What are you doing here?"

Reyes answered without words. He dipped into his

pocket and removed the emerald ring. He placed it on Valenzuela's desk.

Valenzuela's face was immobile except for a small involuntary tic below his right eye. It was a long moment before Valenzuela casually stretched out a hand and folded it around the emerald.

He looked at it carefully, noting the inscribed initials. "Where did you get this?" he asked Mando.

"From Justice. He got—"

"Where did you obtain this, Mr. Justice?" Valenzuela interrupted.

"Colorado."

"That is not much of an explanation, señor."

"You didn't ask for an explanation," Ruff said irritably, "you asked me where I found it."

The tic beneath Valenzuela's eyes increased its tempo. The eyes themselves were obsidian. The servant hovering in the background looked aghast that anyone would speak to the master of the house so sharply. Mando Reyes smiled thinly.

"Then may I have an explanation, señor?" Valenzuela asked with deceptive mildness.

"We can discuss it," Ruff said. He leaned forward, clasping his hands together, "But I've got to say this—I don't like this setup. Mando brought me here against my will. Now I'm cooped in this fortress of yours, surrounded by an army. You're interested in the ring, all right, but what exactly happens to me after I've told you all you want to know?"

Valenzuela managed a laugh. From the sound of it, he hadn't had a whole lot of practice. It was as hearty as a hangman's laugh before he tripped the lever.

"I assure you you are safe in my hacienda. Hospitality and my personal honor demand that any guest be safe in my home."

And once outside? Ruff remarked to himself.

Aloud he said, "Look, I can tell there's something big going on here. To me that ring was a good haul. To a man like you"—Ruff waved a hand around him—"it can't be more than a bauble. So something is up. Mando didn't bring me all the way down here to tell war stories. I want to know what's going on here, and I want to know what's in it for me."

"You are a wise man, Señor Justice." Valenzuela rose and walked to the window, looking through the red velvet drapes into the distances for a minute before turning. "I will tell you everything you wish to know. First, however, you must tell me how you came by the ring."

"All right," Ruff answered after a moment's consideration. He would tell him just enough to keep the man interested. Enough to set the hook.

"I was with a man called Frank Corbett. We were on the run. A bank job had gone all wrong in Leadville."

"Colorado?"

Ruff nodded. "They had practically wiped us out in the streets that day—someone must have talked too much—anyway, there was only the two of us left and we were hard pressed. There was a posse of thirty men on our tails, and we were running toward the high country on horses that were worn down to the nub.

"Winter was coming on, and that was Indian country. But we figured we had to take the chance. No way we were going to outrun that sheriff. We hoped the snows would turn the posse back. That or the Utes.

"We ran as hard and as far as our horses could carry us, then when the horses folded we went on afoot. Winter started to snap at us a little—it snowed, and hard, although it was early May. Winter comes early and stays late in the Rockies."

Valenzuela nodded his comprehension.

"There was snow behind us, and we reckoned that might slow the pursuit. Corbett figured he knew a pass through the mountains that the posse wouldn't know, and if we made it over before it snowed again, we'd be clear of our troubles.

"It didn't sound much good to me. I wasn't dressed for it. Standing there knee deep in snow looking up at those mountains can be intimidating as hell. Finally I gave in and followed Frank up. He said he knew those mountains like the back of his hand—he must not have spent a lot of time looking at his hands."

The servant, at Valenzuela's slight motion, refilled his goblet. Mando shifted impatiently in his chair. Ruff Justice went on.

"We got lost up there when the snow was blowing a fury. We weren't going to make it over a pass that month, and so we went back down, angling south, although that was carrying us right into Ute country and we knew it. Just then we'd rather have taken our chances with the Indians than with the hangman."

"What about the ring?" Mando demanded in exasperation.

"I'm coming to that. I'll cut it short if you prefer. Sometime a week later we was wandering blind. The snows had been heavy and we were out of grub. Frank didn't know where we were, and I didn't either. Looking for a place out of the weather, we came upon this narrow, high-bluffed canyon and we trekked into it. A ways . . . then we stopped cold. It was some kind of Ute burial ground or something.

"There were high cliffs, like I said, and ledges running along them for quite a ways, man-made or natural, I couldn't say. Probably natural, since I never seen any Indians do work like that."

"The ring!" Mando cried out. Valenzuela silenced him with a cold stare.

"There was piles of stone up along these ridges, and a

considerable number of caves cut into the cliffs. We took shelter in one of those caves while the cold winds blew.

"We were all huddled up, froze to the bone, watching the snow drift past the mouth of that high-up cave. Looking around for some wood—the packrats had nested in there and there was twigs, straw and such—"

Mando got up, nearly toppling his chair. He stalked to the window and stared out.

"Go on, Mr. Justice. Mando is an impatient man. It has landed him in serious trouble from time to time."

"Well, I was poking around, and I found it all of the sudden."

"Found what?" Valenzuela asked. His eyes were bright with interest suddenly.

"The cross. Funny damned place for that, but I peered down and sure enough it was a fancy cross with an extra, slantways bar across it. If you looked real close you could see some numbers and something else scratched in the stone."

"What numbers?" Valenzuela asked mildly.

"One seven four zero," Ruff answered.

Valenzuela tried not to show any excitement, but his lean face paled slightly. He turned the goblet in his hands. "And there was writing?"

"Yeah, but I couldn't make it out. It was Spanish and not carved deep. It was dark in the cave, don't forget."

"But you must have been able to make out something."

"Yeah. It said, 'Fortunata,' something like that. It's been a while now, but I recall that. Frank said that it was Spanish and meant a fortune was hidden there. I laughed at him, as I recall. Starving, on the run, he still thought we were going to come out of this wealthy. Frank was like that, an optimist—"

"What did you do?" Valenzuela interrupted this time. Mando had turned, and with hunched, massive shoulders he glared at Ruff from the draped window.

"We poked around. I found a bone. Just the toe of a man or woman—that's all. Funny isn't it?" Ruff smiled thoughtfully. "Anyway, I found the bone, and we worked back into the cave. But it was really dark back there. The walls of the cave leaked water. The floor was ice. The ceiling low. It opened into kind of a room, and then there were six or seven small tunnels running off of it.

"I didn't count on finding no treasure. I didn't even think Frank was translating that 'Fortunata' or whatever it was right. Besides, who hides a treasure and then leaves a sign saying 'This way'?

"I thought that way until I stepped on something that didn't feel like a rock. I hunched down and scooped it up before Frank could see it. It was that ring—you'll notice it's a little bent; that's from me stepping on it."

"Then what did you do?"

"I kept my mouth shut," Ruff said. "Wouldn't you? I convinced Frank it was a wild-goose chase and we gave it up. Next morning was clear and cold. Frank went off to see if he could shoot a deer. We'd decided to hole up in the cave for a time, snow being as deep as it was, not knowing where the posse was. While Frank was gone I made myself a torch and went back in."

"And you found. . . ?"

"Nothing." Ruff shrugged. "I didn't have but an hour. I'd searched the big cave and three of those small tunnels when I heard the shot from outside. I heard another shot on the heels of that one and then half a dozen more.

"Well, Frank didn't need that much lead to stop a deer, so I knew we had trouble. I thought first of the posse, but then I saw the Indians. A mile up the canyon, riding across the snow. I knew what they had."

"Frank Corbett."

"Exactly."

"And what did you do, Mr. Justice?" Valenzuela asked.

"Same thing any sane man would've done. I left out of there at a run. The snow didn't even slow me down. The Utes had me flying across the ground. I got out of the canyon and downslope quick."

"And you never returned?"

"No." Ruff shook his head. "Just then I couldn't, of course. There was a posse and the Utes. I got the hell out of Colorado."

"You could have gone back later."

"Yeah. If I didn't mind the Indians." Ruff smiled thinly. "But I did. Besides, I didn't see anything else in that cave, and I doubted there was anything. Where would it have come from? I wasn't going to risk my hair on a wild chance like that. Though there might have been more. There just might have been. What do you think?"

"One never knows, Mr. Justice," Valenzuela said with a shrug and what was supposed to be a warm smile. He rose from his desk and added, "Now you must be tired."

"Wait. I thought we had a bargain—you were going to tell me what interested you so much in this ring."

"Perhaps another time," Valenzuela said. "For now, rest. You've had a long journey, and it has been a long time since you've been able to sleep in a bed."

Ruff started to object again, but by then another servant had appeared from somewhere and Valenzuela said, "Show Mr. Justice to a guestroom, Pedro."

Ruff went along, hoping that the guestroom wasn't one with bars. It wasn't. Upstairs along a carpeted hallway they entered a large bedroom decorated with the same massive furniture Ruff had seen everywhere. The servant turned down the bed, walked to the balcony, and opened the doors so that a cool wind blew in from off the empty desert. Then with a little bow the man was gone and Ruff was left alone, standing in the luxurious room.

Spanish hospitality. He was a guest in a fine hacienda, his host a cultured Spanish gentleman who only wished for his comfort. Why then was Ruff still wishing desperately that he had a gun?

Little good it would have done him. He walked out onto the balcony and rested his hands on the iron balustrade. The gardens below were silent—the scent of jasmine drifted through the night air. He could make out the shadowy figures of armed men moving along the path. The moon was just rising, spreading an orange glow across the black horizon.

She came into the room silently, and Ruff turned to face Soledad Valenzuela.

8

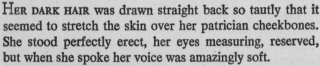

HER DARK HAIR was drawn straight back so tautly that it seemed to stretch the skin over her patrician cheekbones. She stood perfectly erect, her eyes measuring, reserved, but when she spoke her voice was amazingly soft.

"May I speak to you, Mr. Justice?" Her English was almost unaccented. Ruff nodded, and she swept across the room, joining him on the balcony.

"What about?" he asked.

"It is not so easy to begin." She looked away from him, watching the moon rise, pale, bathing the land in golden light.

"Should you be here?" Ruff said.

She waved a hand. "It does not matter."

Ruff didn't quite believe that. Spanish husbands weren't known for letting their women roam around wherever they wished, especially not into strange men's bedrooms. That caused him to wonder if he was being set up here somehow.

"Let's step off the balcony," Ruff suggested. There were too many eyes below.

She followed him without a word. He started to seat himself on the bed, thought better of it, and stood facing Soledad Valenzuela, while she made up her mind to speak.

She began bluntly. "You are not what you pretend, Mr. Justice."

"Oh?" He lifted an eyebrow.

"No, not at all. You are supposed to be a convict, a thug. But I see intelligence in your eyes. That cannot be faked, you know. When you spoke to my husband your words were not quite right. You pretend to be uneducated and very ignorant."

Ruff wondered just how she had overheard him speaking to Ernesto Valenzuela, but he said nothing. She batted long-lashed lids across her deep brown eyes and went on without hesitation.

"Therefore I have hopes that you might be the man."

"The man?"

"The man to take me away from this bastard Valenzuela," she said. Her voice was tight and angry. Then she relaxed, smiling gently.

"I have no idea why you would want to leave your husband," Ruff said evenly, "but I am not the man."

She stepped nearer, and Ruff inhaled a scent of jasmine which was not rising from the gardens below. The lamp at her back painted a halo around her sleek dark hair.

"You think this is a trick, something my husband has designed to test you."

"It occurred to me, yes."

"I assure you it is not." Her voice had dropped to a breathy murmur. Her breasts rose and fell as she spoke.

"When I was twelve years old a gang of bandits burned Rancho Cielo—my father's house. My father, my mother, my grandfather were killed. I was carried away by the leader of the bandit gang."

"Valenzuela?"

"Yes, Ernesto Valenzuela. When I was fifteen he decided to marry me, and I became his wife, loathing him all the time. I could not fight, I could not run. What was there to do? To survive I submitted to the man who had murdered my family."

"Until now."

"Not until now!" She touched her cheek nervously. "I have wanted to kill him since I first saw him, nine years ago, his hands soaked in blood. Once I tried—he beat me and locked me in the cellar for three months.

"I tried to run, but he had me brought back, beaten, and caged again. What was there to do? I had to appear to submit, to forget. I tried to please him. I whispered sweet words into his ears, but when he kissed me I almost gagged at his touch. Still I carried on the masquerade. I haven't the courage to kill myself, señor. I wait and I wait until someone will kill him or take me away. I think maybe you are this man."

"No." Her hand had started to stretch out, to touch his shoulder. It froze in midair and then fell away. Dammit, no one had mentioned a neurotic wife! This could ruin everything. Lovely as she was, she was big trouble. Ruff didn't want to die either. "I guess you read me wrong, lady. Sorry, I'm not the man."

And she left. Turned around and walked regally from the room, leaving Ruff feeling both relieved and cruel. *Was* she telling the truth? What a life she had had. To see her family chopped up and then be forced to marry the man who had done the butchering—if it was true.

Yet Ruff couldn't shake the feeling that she wanted to use him. Maybe Valenzuela had sent her; maybe it was a sort of thrill-seeking game with Soledad. He just didn't know.

Even if he wanted to take her out, it was impossible. There were other people depending on Ruff Justice. Besides, you don't buck an army with your bare hands, not even for the sake of a fair maiden.

Still a vague guilt lingered as he removed his boots and undressed, stretching out on the huge canopied bed. He had enough troubles, he decided suddenly, firmly, and he shoved thoughts of the woman aside, falling to sleep as the moon rose higher, peering in through the balcony window.

The wind whispered in the vine trellis outside his window. At least that's what he thought the sound was until the wind took on form and texture and slid into his bed, warm, whispery, and eager.

"Soledad?"

"Yes, Ruffin Justice."

"Is this some sort of a bribe?"

"No, darling." Her finger ran across his chest. Finding just the right spot, she bent her lips and kissed him there. Her hair was loose now, almost cottony as it fell across him.

Her hands were soft and skillful as they slipped down across his abdomen, over his hard-muscled thighs and hips.

She placed her mouth to his, those supple, caressing lips meeting his warmly. Ruff said something which was muffled by her lips, and she drew her head away.

"If your husband comes around . . ."

"He won't. It's late, very late, and he's fast asleep. A little too much wine, I think." The moonlight was in her eyes. Her lips parted slightly to show her fine white teeth.

"I don't like this a bit, you know?"

"I know, darling." She kissed his throat and placed his hand over her full, firm breast.

"I don't trust you, Soledad."

"I know, darling." She kissed him again, and Ruff gave it up. You can argue only so long with a lady.

She fell against him, her hand going to his crotch, hefting him, stroking him, and he felt her pulse quicken. She was all silky strength, all hips and breasts, buttocks, hungry lips, and he fell into the warm whirlpool of her lovemaking.

Ruff felt her lips run across his abdomen, touch his inner thighs, and his blood began to race furiously.

She sat up, smiling at him, and he let his hand trace the delicate curve of her shoulder, run down her arm and across her breasts, toying with the dark, taut nipples.

"Move over," she said, and he complied. Soledad lay with her face against his pillow, her hips raised, and Ruff positioned himself behind her, his hands running across the incredibly smooth, moon-washed buttocks of Soledad Valenzuela.

He eased forward and felt her hand dart between her legs and search him out. Her hair was spread against the pillow in a dark, silky fan. She was smiling contentedly, lost in sensual speculation.

She positioned him, her hips coming up to devour him, and he entered, feeling her greedy body envelop him, her hand continue to draw him in, to pin him against her warm, pulsing flesh.

The muscles beneath the silky layer of feminine flesh quivered beneath Ruff's hands and she made a tiny, distant gasping sound as he moved up tight against her.

Her hand fell away and her hips began to sway from side to side, gently at first and then turbulently. Ruff clung to her buttocks, trying not to concentrate just yet on the demanding, overwhelming sensations which centered where their bodies were interlocked in fleshy combat.

Soledad's hands clutched the pillow and her thighs quivered as Ruff thrust deeply against the silk of her body. Now she was no longer a rigid, pinned and combed, corseted aristocrat but a savage, catlike creature who lived for sensuality, who was absorbed by it. Her body was a writhing, clutching mass of flesh, small moans, grasping fingertips, fluid and warm, deeply satisfied.

Her head went up and she bit at her lip, her eyes wide as if with astonishment. She held herself arched and still for a moment, her body trembling, and then she sagged against the bed.

Ruff lifted her again and slammed into her, the need growing urgent in his loins. Soledad muttered, *"Sí, sí,"* repetitiously as he brought her rapidly to a second crest where damp, swirling rainbows filled her mind and coursed through her body, becoming hot racing rivers. The man behind her was an animal, yet he was gentle, knowing every bundle of nerves in her body, every contour somehow. She gritted her teeth in concentration and then it exploded again, like fireworks in the night, and she felt that he would drain her, turn her inside out, split her open.

Ruff could hold back no more; he pressed against her, his belly against her buttocks, grasping her pendulous, firm breasts as he reached a climax with a shuddering release.

She rolled over without losing him and they lay face to face, exchanging kisses, her heart beating against Ruff's, her eyes distant. She stroked his back, his buttocks, tangled her fingers in his long, curled hair.

Without intending it, Ruff fell asleep, and when he awoke it was to the rapping of knuckles on his door. He opened his eyes, wondering how he could possibly explain Soledad. But she was already gone, had been gone for hours, apparently. The bed where she had lain was cold, but still a faint scent of her lingered. The sun was rising, the horizon red outside the balcony window. Ruff got to his feet and staggered to the door.

"Breakfast in half an hour, Señor Justice," the servant called through the door, and Ruff muttered a reply.

He returned to the bed and sagged onto it, his head hanging. What now? What had he gotten himself into with this Soledad business?

There were women who would throw it up in their husband's faces. Ruff hoped Soledad wasn't that kind. But then he didn't think people threw anything into the face of Ernesto Valenzuela. Not if they wished to live.

Ruff was still sitting on the edge of the bed, sheet across his lap, when there was another cautious tap at the door. At Ruff's summons the servant poked his head around the door.

"What is it, Pedro?"

"Do you wish a bath, señor?"

It was difficult to imagine anything he wished more. He told Pedro so. Within minutes an ornate zinc tub had appeared and a procession of small servant boys entered, filling the tub with steaming water.

When it was full, Ruff walked to it and slowly, gingerly settled himself into the steaming water, throwing his head back, sighing as the water soaked into aching muscles. The door opened again and Pedro entered. He laid a pair of black trousers and a white silk shirt over a chair, smiled, and went out.

Ruff noticed they had not provided him with a gun.

He soaked for a time, scrubbing down with soft, mildly scented soap. He washed his hair and toweled it, then dressed in the clothes Pedro had left for him.

He went down to breakfast and found Ernesto and Soledad Valenzuela at a table set with silver. Apparently Mando Reyes was not the sort of man one dined with. The big man was absent.

Soledad was an admirable actress. Her eyes showed nothing at all even when Ernesto stared directly at her as if questioning her.

"Sit down, señor, and enjoy your breakfast."

Enjoy it he did. The eggs were scrambled with bits of pepper—both green and red—and two kinds of cheese. There was ham, delicately smoked and honeyed, dark coffee, and sweet caramel rolls.

Soledad kept her eyes from Justice all through the meal. Ernesto had brandy in each of his three cups of coffee, and Ruff wondered just how much the man drank.

Soledad was excused after the meal, and Ernesto Valenzuela took Ruff into a small study, where he offered a cigar.

"I don't smoke," Ruff told him.

"You do not drink and do not smoke." Valenzuela cocked his head in wonder. "One wonders what you do to fill in the idle hours, Mr. Justice." Ruff gave him no answer, and Valenzuela settled himself into a leather chair. "We must now have a serious discussion, Mr. Justice."

"Oh?" Ruff felt his heart skip a beat. The man was going to take the bait. He tried to keep his expression bland and wary.

"Yes." Valenzuela smiled. He was hidden behind a screen of blue cigar smoke. The smoke rose in flat spirals toward the high ceiling.

The sunlight through a high window played on the smoke. Valenzuela leaned forward suddenly. "I told you that I would reveal what I know of the emerald ring you brought to me. Now it is time I do so."

Ruff leaned back in his own chair, hands draped over the arms of his chair, legs crossed. Valenzuela collected himself and spoke.

"You believe you saw the word 'Fortunata' in that cave in Colorado. That is not exactly right. The word was most certainly *Fortuna.*'

"It is the name of a family, a very old and very wealthy family. The man's name was Julio Vargas y Fortuna, at one time a very powerful man in Mexico. In fact his power was greater than that of the Spanish governor, a fact which the governor resented.

"It is a long and interesting chapter in our history, but there is no need to go into it deeply here, Señor Justice. It is enough to say here that in time the governor managed to seize the property and lands of Señor Fortuna. Fortuna was not a man to accept defeat, Justice. He conceived a grand scheme.

"At that time—in the year 1739—North America was sparsely settled. Conflicting claims to territory led to disputes in national capitals, but to no wars—there were no soldiers, Spanish, French, or British, to fight such wars. The truth was, as everyone knew and no one admitted, the lands were held by the Indians."

Pedro appeared without any signal and left a snifter of brandy at Valenzuela's elbow. He sipped from it and went on, waving a cigar as he spoke.

"Julio Vargas y Fortuna commanded a considerable force of men. He had been dispossessed by the Spanish government. He conceived a grand scheme. He would move northward, into the North American wilderness, and establish his own empire. He would be king, and who was there to stop him?

"With his soldiers, and his wife and family, he moved northward, using sixteen wagons to carry his personal belongings, his food stores, and his servants and family. Fifty horsemen rode with him.

"This was on the second day of July in the year 1739. It was the last time Señor Julio Vargas y Fortuna was to be seen. Not one man returned from this expedition, although three horses with the Fortuna brand—a cross with a second, slanted crossbar—were purchased in Santa Fe from two Indians, who when questioned ran away.

"The Señora Fortuna was named Anna Maria," Valenzuela told him, his eyes now intent. "Her wealth was legendary. She was reputed to have more jewels than the Queen of Spain. This is doubtless an exaggeration, but the value of her jewelry was in the millions of pesos."

Ruff was thoughtful, then he suggested the obvious. "The soldiers turned on Fortuna, snatched the jewelry, and took off."

"An acceptable theory, señor . . . if a single piece of

Anna Maria Fortuna's jewelry had ever reappeared. None has. Ever. Until you tried to buy your life with this emerald ring. The initials," Valenzuela said, "are A.M.F. The cross in the cave, the name Fortuna. No, señor, I believe the Indians wiped out the Fortuna party, and I believe Fortuna took shelter in that very cave you described. He would then have had time to hide his valuables."

"Unless the Indians found them."

"I offer the same rebuttal to your theory—none of the jewelry has ever been found."

"Even so," Ruff argued, "it doesn't prove the jewelry is there."

"You speak as though you did not wish to believe it," Valenzuela said. Ruff shrugged.

"It doesn't matter to me what you believe," he said.

"I think it does." Valenzuela rose and perched on the edge of his desk, facing Ruff.

"Why?"

"Because, Justice, I think now that you know what I have told you, you will attempt to go back to this valley of Indian tombs."

"Maybe."

"You would not survive. The Indians would kill you."

"I wouldn't go alone."

"Could you gather fifty men, a hundred? Loyal men who would not cut your throat? I can, Justice. Ernesto Valenzuela can."

Greed shone in those dark eyes. Ruff knew he was hooked. All that was necessary now was to reel him in.

Just get the bastard across the border, Ruff. Then duck, because I'll be waiting with a company of cavalry.

Ruff carried on the pretense. "It could be a wild-goose chase. It's a hell of a long way to go."

"I am not convinced by your reluctance, Justice," Valenzuela said, rising again. He finished his brandy in a swallow. "Let me tell you how it will be!" He leaned forward now, and his face was set, his eyes only slits in his dark face. "I intend to travel to Colorado, I intend to find the Fortuna treasure. You are going with me. As a partner or as a hostage. But you will go with me." His voice was a menacing hiss.

Ruff appeared to consider it. Suddenly he grinned. "When do we leave?"

9

THEY LEFT THE following morning. Valenzuela's expedition wasn't much smaller than Fortuna's must have been. Two wagons carried foodstuffs and ammunition; thirty armed vaqueros awaited Valenzuela's signal to advance. Mando Reyes, appearing sullen and hungover, sat next to Justice. On Ruff's other side was the pockmarked soldier, Ignacio. Pedro, the butler, sat on the seat of one of the wagons, looking miserable. He obviously wanted no part of this, but Valenzuela was not going to be denied any creature comforts. Was that the reason Soledad Valenzuela was along?

For there she was, wearing a buff-colored suit and a straight-brimmed black hat. It was hard for Ruff to figure just why the woman of the rancho was going with them. For Valenzuela's comfort, or because he did not trust her alone at the hacienda? Or had she somehow talked him into taking her?

Ruff saw the sun cresting the horizon, glittering on the dew-frosted hillocks surrounding the Rancho Valenzuela. Valenzuela's hand went up, and the procession started forward, rolling slowly across the broad valley as the sun yellowed and glittered on the stream running across the grasslands.

They were moving, and Ruff breathed a sigh of relief.

It was almost done. It had been a touchy job, hazardous, hinging on certain unpredictable elements. Mando's reaction to the ring—he might have simply killed Ruff and kept it for himself. Valenzuela's reaction—he might have tried to torture Ruff into revealing the location of the valley of tombs. He might not have felt tempted enough to leave his sanctuary.

Instead he had reacted as they had hoped. He was traveling northward toward Colorado. But he would never reach that objective, never find out that there was no valley of golden tombs, that the entire scheme had been constructed by the United States Marshal's office and the army to lure Valenzuela across the border.

Watchers along the border would carry word to Major Harkness, and the cavalry would move in to trap Valenzuela. If the man wasn't shot down during capture, he would hang for his crimes.

"What you think of so many men, Justice? Too much people, too much horses?"

Reyes, sitting a blaze-faced roan, had slippped up beside him. The bandit's face was sleepy, but his eyes were adderlike, threatening.

"It's good," Ruff replied. "The Utes will know we're there if there's five men or fifty. A party this large might keep them off, however."

Mando nodded and drifted away. Dust rose from the wagons as they reached the last of the grasslands. The vaqueros rode silently beneath a hot sun. Ruff Justice let himself relax. There was nothing to the rest of this. A pleasant ride to the border—meals prepared by a chef en route—and then Harkness could write the last chapter.

He shifted in the saddle, saw a dark head peer back toward him and smile. He did not wave to Soledad. He had no intention of lighting the fuse to this powder keg he sat on now. She was a lot of woman, but not worth getting shot over. Ruff looked deliberately away and caught

94

Mando's black eyes on him. The look was one of pure hatred.

Incited by envy, by simple dislike, by who knew what, the man's madness had fixed itself on Ruff Justice, and Ruff frowned, letting his gaze shuttle away.

Maybe Valenzuela had focused Mando's dark instincts on Ruff. There was no way of knowing. One thing Ruff did know—when he was no longer necessary, when the roof fell in, Mando Reyes would try to kill him.

They rolled northward, following the stream until it gave way to the desert. Then they rolled across the empty sands, which bogged the wagons down, across the lava beds and dust-choked playas, the white ball of the sun floating high overhead, beating down on their shoulders and backs.

That evening they camped on the cholla-studded flats. They dined at a table set with linen and crystal, but they were all too weary to speak or to enjoy the roast beef the chef had prepared.

Ruff rolled into his bed beneath the wide-eyed moon, listening to the soft Spanish voices, the distant howl of a mournful coyote.

With the dawn they were moving again, northward and slightly westward, veering away from a course which would lead too near to Tucson. Ruff figured they would cross the international border sometime that afternoon, and by the following day, perhaps, Harkness would be in position to spring the trap.

Ruff tried to figure what he would do then. Mando and Ignacio had obviously been assigned to watch him, and he was weaponless.

Well, there was no planning for it. The only advantage he had was that he knew what was coming while Valenzuela's forces didn't. He would have to stay alert and take his chances, and at the first sign of the cavalry column, or the first shot, dig his heels just as far into the belly of that buckskin as he could.

The day was as hot and as dry and as dusty as the one preceding it. No one spoke. Their tongues were swollen in their mouths. The horses hung their heads miserably.

At four o'clock that afternoon, Ruff looked up, measured his landmarks, and figured they were into United States territory. He felt himself relax slightly. He hadn't realized how tight he was. Now he felt the knots in his shoulders loosen. He took a slow deep breath, repressed a smile, and glanced at Mando Reyes, finding his eyes as dark and deadly as ever.

"I thought we were *amigos,* Mando! What's the matter?"

Reyes muttered something and turned his eyes away. Ignacio took over his glaring for him.

They lost a wheel off one of the wagons fording a dry streambed, and Soledad had to step down and wait while the soldiers repaired it. She stood in the scant shade of a mesquite bush, her dark eyes on Ruff Justice, a faint smile curving those lips which Ruff recalled so well.

What caused him to turn his head he couldn't have said, but turn it he did, and he found himself confronted by Ernesto Valenzuela.

His eyes were smoldering, and his mouth oddly triumphant. Before Ruff could say anything, the bandit king had turned and he walked away. Ruff glanced at Soledad again. She watched him with amusement. Smiling broadly, she turned her back to Justice.

So he knew. Somehow he knew. Soledad had told him perhaps, or his servants. But he knew. Maybe that was why Soledad was along. Perhaps he intended to leave her in the vast Colorado wilderness. Side by side with her lover.

They rolled on across the empty land throughout the

afternoon, and now there was no longer any doubt—they were in the United States.

If the vaqueros were nervous, they showed none of it. But then most of them had been across before—butchering and looting, burning their way across the territory.

The land had changed again. It was white sand and massive pipe-organ cactus. They cast long shadows before a dying sun.

Ruff gratefully stepped from the buckskin and unsaddled. No one came to call him to supper when Valenzuela ate, and it was just as well.

Ruff ate what the other men ate—roast beef and cold tortillas, washed down with as much water as he could hold.

He sat near his horse in the twilight, eating silently. But he was not alone. Reyes was eating his own meal not ten feet from Justice.

"I kill you pretty soon, Justice," Mando said as if commenting on the weather. "Pretty soon you will be dead. What you think of that?"

Ruff said nothing. Pretty soon someone would be dead, many men perhaps. Harkness had had time to get the word that Valenzuela had crossed the border, had had time to mount his force and was even now closing behind the bandit army.

Someone would die. And perhaps Mando was right—maybe it was Ruff Justice himself who would go down first. But like most men, Ruff found it impossible to comprehend his own death; like most men, deep inside, he considered himself immortal. That didn't keep him from giving deep consideration to the business of staying alive.

He had no worries about that as long as Valenzuela needed him, that is, until they found the valley of golden tombs. But the instant Valenzuela realized that this was a trap, Ruff Justice would be cut down.

He needed a gun, and now. Harkness, if on schedule,

would hit the bandits in the morning, or in the afternoon at the latest.

He rolled up in his blanket and pretended to sleep, knowing that eyes were watching. The hours passed slowly, the stars dragging past through the inky sky. It was only an hour before dawn when Ruff moved.

Mando was nearby still, leaning up against the wagon wheel. His hat was low over his eyes, his rifle across his lap. The starlight showed plainly that those eyes were closed.

Ruff slowly rolled out of his bed, his eyes on Mando each moment. He got to a crouch and then stood, walking in bare feet away from his bed.

A mounted guard passed nearby, and Ruff pressed himself into the shadows of a pipe-organ cactus, standing motionless as the bandit rode by. Then he moved, and quickly.

He had already decided whose gun he wanted. Someone who would likely be careless in watching it, someone who alone among this crew might be reluctant to report it missing. He slipped to the rear of the cook's wagon.

Pedro slept curled in a ball on top of two sacks of flour. Ruff glanced around at the dark desert and slipped inside, his bare feet noiseless as he crept across the wagon bed.

He found the gun hanging on a peg and slipped it from its holster. Quickly then he went to the rear of the wagon. He was about to step out when he heard a whispered voice. He drew back inside the wagon flap quickly, holding the pistol beside his ear.

The minutes passed with incredible slowness. The sun would be rising soon and Ruff would be caught, but finally the two guards wandered off. Ruff slipped from the wagon and returned to his bed.

Everything had gone smoothly. Mando seemed still to

be asleep; Ruff had the pistol tucked into his waistband behind his loose-fitting white shirt.

He had just reached his bed and was starting to crawl into it when Mando's voice boomed out.

"Just a minute, hombre! What are you up to, huh?"

The big man was to his feet. He ambled toward Ruff, who was rolling up his bed now as if it had been his intention all along.

"It's nearly dawn." Ruff shrugged. "Time to get up."

He tied his roll and left it. Walking to his buckskin, he slipped the bit into its reluctant mouth and patted its neck.

Mando watched him with hooded eyes as Ruff led the horse to the portable trough Valenzuela had brought along to water the stock.

Ruff could feel the dark eyes of the bandit, like little sabers, scoring his back, but Mando said nothing more.

Breakfast was more cold beef and black coffee. By the time the sun was fully up they were moving northward once more. Pedro had said nothing about the gun, apparently, and Ruff was feeling better about things. Now at least he had a chance. And today was the day that Harkness planned to hit the bandit caravan.

But he didn't that morning, and Ruff rode with a growing impatience in him, his eyes searching the flat horizon, watching for the first sign of dust against the pale sky. There was none.

And as afternoon faded to evening and they began to enter the broken hills overgrown with sage and manzanita, Ruff's frown deepened.

Maybe he had been wrong about Harkness' target day. Maybe the major had been detained or had decided—logically—that there was better cover in the hills for an advancing army. But as the wagons halted near a sundown-reddened gorge, Ruff knew that Harkness would not hit them that day. His expectations had been wrong.

He had been wrong about another matter.

They marched up to him as camp was being set up. Valenzuela, Mando, Ignacio, and a shaken Pedro. He had told them about the gun.

Valenzuela walked directly to Ruff and slammed his fist into his jaw. Ruff went sprawling and barely managed to roll away from a kick aimed at his head. He came to his feet panting.

"Where is the gun, hombre?" Valenzuela asked. There was none of the Spanish gentleman in his manner now. He was simply a cold-eyed, hatchet-faced killer.

"What gun?" Ruff tried, but they weren't buying that offering. Valenzuela's fist slammed into his face again, and Ruff felt hot blood trickle from his nostril.

"Give us the gun. You do not need it, Justice. We will protect you."

Ignacio laughed. Mando stood back a step or two, his big fists clenching and unclenching. The son of a bitch was just waiting for his master to turn him loose to maul and tear, to kill.

There was no point in denying it any longer. He couldn't conceal the gun, couldn't shoot them all. He shrugged indifferently and withdrew it, handing it to Valenzuela.

"Keep it with you from now on, *idiota*," Valenzuela said sharply, slapping the gun in Pedro's hand. Pedro bowed and scraped away, and Valenzuela nodded to Mando, whose eyes lit up with malicious glee.

Valenzuela turned sharply on his heel and strode away. Mando was taking off his gunbelt, moving in. Ruff watched him, knowing that this beating was not for the gun. It was for Soledad.

Mando was big, tough, and confident, but Valenzuela was taking no chances. Ignacio was also taking off his gunbelt. He looked no less happy about it than Mando did.

Mando was impatient. He was to Justice first, throwing a wild right hand with all of his oxlike power behind it. The punch was powerful but not accurate. Ruff stepped inside of the punch, driving his own fist into Mando's wind. The big man blinked with surprise and backed off, holding his gut.

He didn't back off for long. With a roar Mando came in again. This time he didn't worry about boxing; he piled into Ruff and they tumbled to the earth together, Ruff clinging to the big man's greasy hair.

Ruff hit hard, Mando's weight forcing the breath from him in a gasp. He shoved an awkward right into Mando's face, but he didn't have the leverage to do any damage with it. Mando hooked a right to Ruff's ribcage and then another before Ruff managed to bring his long legs up, hook Mando's chin, and yank him over backward.

Ruff got to his feet facing Mando, who was cursing loudly, wildly. Ignacio had decided it was time to jump in, and he did, with both feet.

Leaping at Ruff, the bandit slammed an elbow into Justice's cheek, spinning his head around. Ruff saw that Ignacio kept his chin up and he countered with a forearm shot to Ignacio's windpipe.

The bandit fell away, gagging and clutching his throat, but Mando was back, all over Ruff with swarming punches thrown with either hand.

Ruff had to back away from the barrage, pausing once to kick out at Mando's kneecap.

The kick was well aimed. Ruff's bootheel caught the bandit flush on the knee. It should have sent him to the ground with a broken kneecap or at least halted him through sheer pain, but Mando Reyes barely flinched.

He came in hard now, and the bandit army which had gathered around in the twilight cheered as Mando caught Ruff with a crushing right-hand shot to the shelf of the jaw. Ruff somehow shook it off and came in again, his anger high.

He jabbed twice, three times in succession to Mando's head, snapping it back, bloodying the big man's nose, pulping his lips, but Mando didn't back up. He bored in, madness showing in his eyes.

Still Ruff managed to hold him off, taking a right-hand hook on his shoulder, slipping a left as he jabbed and then crossed with a stiff hook of his own. But Ignacio, roaring like a bull, had rejoined the fray.

Mando winged a left which Ruff ducked, but Ignacio, behind Ruff, drove a crippling shot to Ruff's kidney, and Justice sagged, his knees buckling under him. He was halfway down when Reyes, grinning with bloody triumph, lifted Ruff to his toes with an uppercut which came from the ground.

Ruff staggered back—into the arms of Ignacio.

Ignacio's arm went around Ruff's throat and clamped tight. Ruff threw an elbow back and kicked at Ignacio's shin, but the bandit kept his strangling grip. Now Mando had moved in, and he pounded at Ruff's body with triphammer punches. The lights went on in Ruff's skull.

For a moment he fought back desperately, getting a right up and into Mando's ugly face. Then Ignacio's stranglehold and the battering punches of Mando Reyes took their toll, and Ruff couldn't fight back the darkness as he gasped for breath.

He felt himself going limp, felt Mando hammering away at his ribs, felt Ignacio choking the breath from him. He saw the ring of dark bandits' faces, their mouths open in soundless cheering. Then the world cartwheeled once and turned crimson.

He was lying on the ground. Ignacio had let go. Mando was hovering over him, still cursing, and as Ruff watched the big man produced a long-bladed skinning knife. Ruff tried to move away but could not, and Mando got to his knees, his face distorted by madness, his eyes glittering. His knees were on Ruff's shoulders, pinning him, and he had the knife at Ruff's throat.

"No, Mando!" Ignacio shouted.

He shouted it again, endlessly, as Mando yanked Ruff's head up by the hair and placed the cold edge of the knife against Ruff's throat.

"No, Mando!" Ignacio's voice was nearly panicked. He shouted to the others, and two bandits came forward, dragging Mando Reyes off. Mando stood, his barrel chest rising and falling, his knuckles white as he gripped the knife. His hair hung in his face; he worked his teeth together. A drop of spittle sparkled on the corner of his savage mouth.

Then he turned and was gone. Ruff was left to lie where he had fallen as the sky went dark. He lay there peering through a swollen eyelid at the stars, his body aching, his head hammering with pain. He closed his eyes, and then darkness fell completely.

When he awoke it was to the pain of jolting along across the searing desert, tied belly down across the saddle of his buckskin. With each step of the horse Ruff felt like vomiting. He did.

Reyes' braying laugh filled his ears. By craning his neck he was able to make out the lumpy, dark face of the bandit.

"How you like that, Ruffin Justice? You lucky, hombre. Ignacio hadn't stopped me I would have given you a new mouth—on your throat!"

Finding himself charmingly amusing, Reyes broke into a horsy laugh. Ruff vomited again.

At noon the great man himself appeared as they halted at an arroyo crossing. Valenzuela yanked Ruff's head up by the hair and spat into his face.

"I'm running out of patience with you, Justice. If I didn't need you, you'd be dead. Twice over. You be a good boy and I'll let you ride in the saddle. Well?" he demanded.

Ruff nodded weakly, and from somewhere Mando's laugh sounded again. Someone cut him loose, and Ruff slid from the horse's back to land roughly against the earth.

He got to hands and knees and looked up to see Valenzuela sitting his black horse like some feudal lord. An anger rose in Ruff, like a sheet of flame, and he almost did it—he almost leaped at the Mexican, wanting to tear his throat out. But he managed to fight it back.

He got to his feet and leaned against the steaming, sweaty flank of the buckskin, his head on his forearm.

When he peered up again, Valenzuela was gone. Mando, his face oddly sullen as he went through another of his rapid mood changes, was watching.

"He means it, hombre. He will kill you. Or maybe just let you ride all the way to Colorado tied to your horse. You get smart, Ruffin Justice. Hear me?"

Ruff nodded weakly. He climbed up into the saddle, wiping his hair back. There was a dry wind gusting down the gravel-bottomed arroyo. The sun was high in the sky.

Ruff looked to the broken hills around them. A patchwork of crumbling low mesas, bluffs, and brush-clotted barrancas. An army could be hidden out there.

But where was the army? Harkness was a day overdue. Ruff, battered and weary, but on edge with anticipation, followed the others through the arroyo and up onto a broad plateau where dry gramma grass grew in patches, where their party startled a feeding mule deer which bounded away and lost itself in the maze of canyons.

Where was Harkness?

They plodded on. In late afternoon the shadows ran out from the base of the hulking mesa to their left. The land had changed again. Now they found scattered pine and much manzanita. They had gained altitude and as a result it had been cooler through the long afternoon.

Ruff ate silently, chewing with some difficulty. His jaw was swollen, his tongue lacerated. He turned in and slept like the dead.

The prodding of a boot toe brought him back to life. The sun was a fierce red ball glaring through the pines along the high ridge to the east.

Ruff ate sullenly, slowly, and an hour later they broke camp. That day they crossed the Little Colorado, and still there was no Harkness. There was only Ruff Justice and the bandits, the empty goal of the valley of golden tombs, the broad land.

They skirted the Painted Desert and continued north by east. It rained the next day. A brief cloudburst which barely settled the dust. The clouds had cleared away by evening. They camped on a low knoll near Steamboat Canyon.

The vaqueros were weary. Twice they had done battle among themselves. One man had been knifed. And Harkness had not come.

"Soon we be in Colorado, huh, Ruffin Justice?" Mando asked eagerly.

Ruff only nodded. The big man was pleased. The sooner they were in Colorado, the sooner Mando could give himself the pleasure of killing Justice. There was no doubt that death was the ultimate fate Valenzuela had planned for him.

Day followed weary day, and still Harkness did not appear. And now Ruff knew he would not. Fort Thomas was far to the south. The moment had come and then gone. Something had gone wrong.

Ruff tried to figure what it was, but he couldn't come up with a good guess. Well, he thought bitterly, everything had gone right up until the crucial moment.

He had gotten himself into prison, made contact with

Mando Reyes, escaped with the big bandit and been taken to his chieftan. Valenzuela had taken the bait and left his Mexican stronghold to enter the United States where he could be arrested and hung.

Everything had gone as planned—until now.

Slowly the realization came to Ruff. There would be no help. Not today, not the next day. It was all up to him. It was almost funny, but Ruff didn't smile. It was up to him to arrest fifty armed men and take Valenzuela in to face the charges against him, to battle men like Mando Reyes and Ignacio without a weapon.

It was absurd, insane. It was also the only choice.

If he did nothing they would ride to Colorado, and there Ruff would be killed. Valenzuela would suffer only the inconvenience of a long, fruitless ride. He would return to Mexico to never pay for his crimes.

Then how? Ruff's mind was made up. He would have his try. That left only the question, *how?* How do you attack an army with bare hands? It would take some pondering, and there was little enough time even for planning. Ruff had known all morning that the party had entered Colorado.

10

······──◆──······

THE VAST FORMS of the Rocky Mountains began to loom against the sky. Still distant, purple, streaked with the white of everlasting snow, they grew larger with each passing mile.

Ruff had formulated plan after plan, each of them as farfetched as the one preceding it. Finally he was left with only one seemingly plausible idea. He would have to wait until the last moment, and it was chancy in more than one way, but he had begun to believe it might work—possibly because he had no other chance.

His fable had placed the valley of tombs near Leadville. He would have to wait until they were within a few miles of that town before he made his try. If he could shake free of the outlaws and ride to Leadville, word could be sent to the nearest army post, Fort Vasquez up along the South Platte. Once the army had been informed, a telegraph message could be sent to Fort Thomas and the border sealed off. Instead of trapping Valenzuela on his way into the United States, he could be captured trying to leave.

If. If he could shake loose. If he could make Leadville without being shot or ridden down. But there was no other way. None at all that occurred to him.

They wound through the foothills, moving toward the

high country, and the winds grew cold. They scattered a herd of elk, and Valenzuela took one down at four hundred yards with his .45-90. Justice had the idea it was a demonstration. He got the message.

They camped on a high bluff that night, and there was grumbling among the men. They were at six thousand feet and climbing. The wind shrieked up the canyons and knifed through their clothing. Mando sulked, his mood heavy and somber. Soledad, silent and mechanical herself, wore a hooded fur coat as she sat brooding, staring at the blazing campfire. She was one of the few who had brought warmer garments. The bandits cursed, stamped their feet, and slapped themselves.

"Why didn't you tell me it was this cold up here?" Valenzuela demanded of Justice.

"I didn't want to insult your intelligence," Ruff replied.

Valenzuela, muttering, stalked away. Ruff poured himself a cup of coffee from the gallon pot and replaced it near the fire.

Soledad, who had ignored him for days, was watching him, and she said, "Come sit here, Mr. Justice."

Ruff looked around. He could see nothing outside the ring of fire, but he believed Valenzuela had gone to the wagon. Mando was nowhere to be seen. He nodded and sat by her.

"What is it, Señora Valenzuela?"

"You have not come near me, Ruff."

"I had enough troubles," he responded. He sipped his coffee.

"I know. I hate him!" she said, her eyes flashing.

Ruff answered with a tiny shrug. He watched her face by firelight, amazed at the delicate structure of the bones, the flawless skin, the smoothly curved lips. She was pouting now, emphasizing the bee-stung fullness of her lower lip.

"What I told you before . . ." she hesitated. "All of it

was true, Ruff Justice. The things he's done to me. And now . . ." She glanced toward the wagon, hidden in shadow, "After the treasure is found, he will kill you."

"I know it."

She registered surprise. She leaned nearer and added, "And he will kill me. He has told me this already, boastingly. It is the truth. Ernesto Valenzuela does not say things he does not mean, Ruff Justice."

"And so?" Ruff finished the coffee. It had been scalding when he poured it, but now it was already cold.

"And so!" She laughed, painfully. "I don't want to die, Ruff. I don't want to live—with him." Her hand rested briefly on his wrist, and her eyes, dark and fire-bright, met his.

"I'm helpless," he answered. What game was the lady playing now?

"With a gun you would not be helpless."

"I tried that—remember?"

"Yes. But suppose I had a gun. Then who would know I had given it to you? You could protect us, Ruff. You could kill him first."

Her eyes were eager, and Ruff wondered again at the motives of this darkly beautiful woman. But a gun—it was an offer he couldn't turn down.

"You have it with you?"

She nodded and drew her sleeve up an inch or so, and Ruff could see the dull gleam of a pistol hidden there. It was a little Smith & Wesson pocket .32, not a lot of gun, but it beat throwing rocks at them.

"Leave it behind the log," Ruff said. "Then go."

Soledad nodded. She reached into her sleeve, leaning near enough to whisper "Kill him!" fiercely into Ruff's ear. Then she negligently placed the pistol behind the skinned log they were sitting on, rose, and walked away, her hips swaying with slight, effective emphasis.

Ruff waited a time, and when he was sure no eyes were

on him, he dropped a hand behind the log, scooped up the pistol, and stuffed it into his pocket. The loads he would check later.

He watched her until she was swallowed up by the shadows, and he wondered. What were her real motivations? Ruff didn't trust her; he couldn't afford to. But she was a complication, another factor in the already difficult equation which had to be considered.

Two new complications presented themselves the next morning. Ruff opened his eyes to a gray, blustery dawn. It was dark, and the wind was raging up the canyon. The first snowflakes began falling shortly after breakfast.

"It can't snow," Mando shouted to all who would listen. "It's too early for it."

Too early in Mexico, perhaps, but Ruff had seen it snow early and hard in the Rockies on many occasions. He didn't mind it in the least, although he had only his buckskin jacket. It would make for hard going if it kept up, and for poor visibility. A man could get lost in a snowstorm.

It didn't snow hard, but it was steady throughout the morning as Ruff led them higher and higher into the mountains, across snow-glazed valleys and through high timber.

"How far?" Valenzuela kept demanding impatiently. The snow was in their faces. Valenzuela's lips were blue. "How much higher up, Justice?"

"Quite a ways still. Quite a ways."

"If this is some crazy idea of yours, Justice, some trick, I'll kill you, you know that, don't you?"

"I know it," Ruff said, and he looked at Valenzuela. Valenzuela looked back, and perhaps for the first time he saw the steely depths of that ice-blue gaze of Ruff Justice, and for the first time he had his doubts about the man.

"Remember it," he said, wheeling his black horse away, and Ruff Justice, watching him go, smiled thinly.

"I'll remember it, Señor Valenzuela," he whispered. As if he could forget it.

They rode on and the snow continued. The road got rougher and then vanished as they topped an eight-thousand-foot-high ridge and overlooked a deep, wind-washed canyon.

The wind whipped Ruff's hair and the fringes of his buckskin jacket. It jabbed icy fingers into his face, and he shivered. If the snow kept up they did have a problem, and it was as much his problem as Valenzuela's. There would be very little satisfaction in knowing the others were suffering the same fate as he froze to death.

He had to get lower, he had to make his break. Leadville was eight tangled miles away, Ruff guessed. If it had been clear they might be able to see it from where they now sat. But it was not clear. The stormclouds rolled across the land, blotting out the sun.

It had to be soon, while the storm still covered for him, but Mando and Ignacio seemed to stick tighter to him than ever.

They lost the first wagon a mile on. The axle gave way fording a whitewater freshet and the supplies had to be emptied out. The second wagon lasted another quarter of a mile. The trail Ruff had been following turned sharply upward, winding between rocky cliffs which pinched off the road until there was room enough only for a man on horseback.

"Dammit, isn't there another way?" Valenzuela fumed.

"Not that I know of," Ruff said dryly. "Of course, we could cast about a bit. If you want me to go out and scout around . . ."

"Pedro! Saddle a horse for my wife!" Valenzuela turned away and stalked back through the swirling blue snow. Ruff smiled. Small cracks were beginning to appear in the man's composure. As Justice watched, Valenzuela went to the rear of the wagon and withdrew a bottle of whiskey. He drank a third of it without taking the bottle from his lips.

Soledad appeared, looking sleepy and uncomfortable, and was helped down from the wagon. While Pedro saddled her horse the second wagon was unloaded. The vaquero's horses were now loaded down with extra, mostly useless gear. Bedding, cookstoves, tables, and silver utensils hung from their horses.

Ruff watched expressionlessly until the voice at his ear said, "Think you're a pretty smart fellow, don't you, Mr. Ruffin Justice? Watching everything go to hell. Let me tell you, hombre, treasure, no treasure, Valenzuela, no Valenzuela, soon Mando will kill you. I do not joke."

Ruff didn't think Mando was joking. He watched the big man ride slowly toward the wagon. Some of the soldiers had hooked their ropes onto the wagon and were preparing to roll it over and off the trail.

That done, they clanked on, the vaqueros grim, Valenzuela sullen, Mando murderous. It continued to snow, but already Ruff had adjusted his plan to the weather and found that this complication suited him.

The other one didn't. It sent cold chills up his spine.

It was Ignacio who found them, and he halted the party, lifting a hand. Valenzuela and Justice rode forward to where Ignacio was crouching. He looked up at them, pointing at the ground.

You could still see them clearly in the snow. Six or seven unshod horses had passed this way not more than an hour before. The Utes were prowling.

They rode warily after that, but their passage could hardly go unnoticed. Each unexpected cloud shadow or landform appearing from out of the storm caused nerves to tighten.

"You could dump that junk we're carrying," Ruff told Valenzuela.

"What do you mean?"

"All that clattering and clanking," Ruff told him. "The family silver, the tables—we're just making sure they can hear us even farther than they can see us, and that's saying something. We can't hide fifty men, but we can try to use some sense."

"It makes no difference," Valenzuela believed. "The Indians will not try to attack us. We are too many."

"Maybe, maybe so in a head-on confrontation, but they can pick us off one by one as we pass through the forests or ride under a cliff, as we try to ford a river. And your men are hampered by their extra load. They know it, Valenzuela. I might be wrong—maybe you know them better than I do—but it seems to me a man might grow a little resentful, carrying all your treasures. Not only that, you're tiring the horses unnecessarily."

"I said it does not matter!" Valenzuela shouted.

It mattered a mile on. The vaquero toppled silently from his saddle and no one had a hint that anything was wrong until they saw him go, until they rolled him over and found the Ute arrow in his back.

"Where are they?" Valenzuela rode in a half circle. Men bristled with guns. The snow washed down. Valenzuela shouted meaningless orders and had his men form up into a defensive box.

Poised like that they sat out the hours while the snow fell, adding to the two feet already on the ground. It was growing dark and still nothing had happened. Nothing would, Ruff knew. It would be that way from here on out—a man picked off as he watered his horse, as he slept. And there was nothing on earth to be done about it.

Except to turn back, and Valenzuela would never do that. His eyes glittered like gold when he spoke of the golden tombs. He must have dreamed of the Fortuna treasure at night. He had all a man could want already, but then those are the men to whom money matters the most.

They rode still higher until darkness and the storm made it impossible to travel farther. Then they sat hunched around the tiny red cones of their campfires, trying to stay warm, to fight off their fears.

Twenty men stood guard at once, but Ruff knew that even that was not enough if the Utes wanted to strike. They could sift like cloud shadows through the picket line and strike whenever they wished.

The storm broke sometime after midnight and the stars came out, frozen, brilliant. The snow glimmered with starlight, the world was an icy, crystal wonderland. Even the wind had ceased, and the sounds of men walking across the snow were loud, audible for miles.

It was time. Ruff had decided after supper. It was time to get the hell out of there, to make his try. With luck, if he could get a decent lead, he could beat them to Leadville—assuming the Utes cooperated.

Valenzuela was growing unstable, Mando was sullen and anxious. Ruff had only to choose his time. At the first opportunity he was going to take his chance.

He lay back watching the stars. They were gradually being devoured by new clouds. It would snow again. He closed his eyes, trying to sleep. He would need the rest.

Morning was gray and somber. They ate without speaking. Ruff noticed that the vaqueros' horses were lighter now. They had been dumping Valenzuela's goods when no one was watching. If Valenzuela cared he made no comment.

They saddled and rode slowly on. The snow was to a horse's knees now and the wind biting. They followed a high ridge trail which snaked along the face of the sheer gorges where white water rushed seaward. Justice was in the lead now with his bodyguards—Mando and Ignacio—close behind. There was room for only one horse at a time here on the icy, treacherous trail.

The wind gusted up the gorge and clawed at them. The

skies had been lowering all morning, and now it began to snow again.

Ruff kept his eyes moving, searching the trail ahead. Now, rounding a tight bend, he found what he wanted. The bend in the trail was shaped like a horseshoe, and midway through the bend a gully cut across their path.

Timber grew down to the trail, and once into that a man would have a chance of getting himself lost permanently.

Ruff swiveled in his saddle. Mando was close behind, the rest of the party strung out for half a mile down the hairline trail. Now the clouds began to drop more snow—light, fleecy at first, but within minutes it was a swirling wash.

Mando's eyes caught him, but Ruff said nothing. He simply turned in the saddle and continued. The clouds screened him from Mando briefly, and Ruff urged the buckskin into a trot.

"Hey! Not so fast!" Mando called out. But he was calling blindly. There was no way he could see Justice through the clouds and snow. The trail underfoot was heavy with snow, glazed with ice under that, but Ruff lifted his buckskin into a canter, wanting to put the distance between himself and Mando Reyes.

He had nearly made it to the timber when the clouds cleared briefly and a raging shout went up from Mando Reyes. Ruff turned and saw Mando and Ignacio spurring their ponies along the trail, heard the whip of a bullet as it flew past his ear followed by the sharp, flat report of the rifle.

Ruff ducked low across the withers of his buckskin and whipping it with the reins he drove it upslope, into the pines.

Bullets sang into the woods. The bark of a spruce beside Ruff's head was torn away, exposing the white meat. Ruff urged his horse on, winding his way upslope, the bullets flying wildly through the timber.

He ducked under a low-hanging limb, skirted a jumble of snow-covered boulders, and then rode downslope. He was within a hundred feet of the trail, not a quarter of a mile from where he had entered the woods. He could clearly see the pursuit following his tracks upslope.

Ruff smiled to himself and began riding parallel to the trail and southward, back in the direction from which they had come. Behind him an occasional shout went up, and once a shot which must have been aimed at a ghost.

They would pick up his trail eventually, but they wouldn't be able to follow it far or fast in this snow. Ruff angled his buckskin toward higher ground. He was a hundred feet or so above the trail, and it was an almost sheer drop. There were twenty vaqueros sullenly sitting their horses there, waiting for orders while the rest of the party scoured the woods.

Suddenly there was a shot from below, and it came too near, much too near. Ruff was out of the timber briefly, and the clearing clouds had given him away. A second shot followed on the heels of the first, and then the roar of guns was like thunder.

Fortunately, it was a tough shot, upslope from horseback, and the bullets missed—some by not much. Ruff leaped from the buckskin and got behind it, walking the rearing, kicking animal upslope, his own legs buried to the knees in snow.

He found the dead trees and then the pile of boulders, and the deadly idea came to him.

There was enough snow on that ridge to make it work. It was murderous and ugly, but he was mad enough just then not to care. They were trying to kill him, every man jack of them, and for pay. They would snuff out a man's life for a few dollars, clean their guns, and discuss it around the campfire while they smoked and told jokes.

The anger which had been smoldering in Ruff now flared up, and he got to work. Breaking a limb from a deadfall, he dug through the snow beneath a mamoth, gray boulder, and he heaved. Nothing happened, although his muscles popped and his legs began to tremble with the strain. The bullets whined all around him, one of them kicking stone dust into his face, and behind the pursuit was closing.

Finally something gave. The boulder came loose of its ancient moorings, canted up, and slowly rolled over. For an instant Ruff thought it would settle again, but it turned again, slowly.

Then it began to pick up momentum. A shout went up from below and the shooting stopped as the men shouted and tried to ride their horses past other men on the narrow trail. It was impossible to turn a horse, impossible to hide. Where could they run?

The boulder knocked loose a stack of smaller rocks and then bounded high into the air, slowly turning. When it hit again the snow started to move with it, and soon it seemed the whole mountain was sliding, racing toward the bottomless gorge below.

The avalanche creaked and groaned and then sounded like a dozen locomotives as tons of snow and rock slid off the mountain, the entire ledge going.

And below that through the snow dust, through the clouds, Ruff Justice could see the frantic horses rearing, see the wild-eyed expressions of the trapped vaqueros, see them swept over into the yawning gorge, their horses cartwheeling through space, the panicked sounds they made overwhelmed by the roaring of the thundering avalanche.

A shot from behind him caused him to duck low and dart for the buckskin before the snow had settled. He had the horse running before he had hit the saddle and now he was into the timber again, weaving his way upslope, the guns echoing behind him.

He could see Mando, his rifle leveled, see the puff of smoke from the muzzle of his Sharps rifle, and moments later the report sounded.

There were six or seven men spread out behind him, racing recklessly upslope. Now was the time to show them he had some teeth. It would slow them down some, breed some caution.

Ruff put the brakes to the buckskin and yanked the little .32 from his waistband. He two-handed it, taking a half breath and holding it as he squeezed the trigger. All the same he was surprised to score a hit at that distance with the little pea shooter.

But he was no more surprised than the man with the red scarf who rode beside Mando Reyes must have been when the bullet slammed into his chest, jarring him from the saddle.

The bandits held up in momentary confusion and then made for the shelter of the timber themselves.

Ruff didn't waste another shot. He turned his horse and rode on, riding upslope and then backtracking a way until he took up his true course, a southeasterly angle which, with luck, would lead him eventually to Leadville.

An hour passed and then another during which he saw no pursuit, heard nothing but the wind which drove the constant snow down. He was beginning to grow confident, perhaps too confident. He didn't see the Ute warrior until it was too late.

11

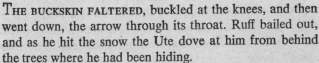

THE BUCKSKIN FALTERED, buckled at the knees, and then went down, the arrow through its throat. Ruff bailed out, and as he hit the snow the Ute dove at him from behind the trees where he had been hiding.

Ruff's hand dropped for the butt of the Smith & Wesson in his waistband, but before he could bring it up the Indian slammed into him and they tumbled to the snow, the pistol flying free.

Ruff saw the bronzed face, the sleek dark hair, saw the look of savage triumph all in the instant they collided.

The brave had him pinned and his right arm was lifted high, the long-bladed knife gleaming dully as it arced downward. Ruff slammed out with a forearm and rolled his head away. The knife barely missed, burying itself in the snow.

Ruff fought back savagely, but the brave was all over him. The man had incredible strength and he was cat-quick.

As Ruff tried to hook him with a heel the warrior ducked low and slashed at Ruff's throat with the knife. Ruff managed at the last moment to get hold of the Ute's wrist, deflecting the blow, but still he almost took it in the throat.

With the strength of desperation Ruff hooked a chopping right hand to the Ute's neck and the warrior was knocked from Justice's chest. Ruff rolled aside, the Indian lunging, hacking down with his knife. Ruff felt it tear through his buckskin jacket. He kept rolling, then came to his feet.

The warrior was already to his, and he came in, knife held low, circling Justice. Ruff glanced around him, searching for the pistol, not finding it. The buckskin lay against the snow, its blood steaming from its throat.

The Ute leaped at Ruff. Justice stepped aside and tripped him. The warrior went down, rolling to his back, knife poised before Ruff could take advantage of it.

Justice backed away, still looking for the pistol, but it was lost beneath the snow. The Ute was on him again, and the knife slashed low, drawing a thin red line across Ruff's belly as he jerked away. Ruff kicked out and missed, kicked out again and caught the young warrior full in the groin.

The Ute folded up, and Ruff went in. The knife cut out at him awkwardly, and Ruff slapped it away with his left hand. His right locked on the Ute's wrist, and they went down in a heap.

Ruff put his forearm over the Ute's throat and mashed down, and only then did he realize the Indian was no longer struggling.

He still had the wrist in his hand, and now he looked down to where the bloody knife protruded from the Indian's belly. The Ute was dead.

Slowly Ruff rose, his breath coming in icy puffs. His hair was in his eyes, and he wiped it back. He yanked the knife from the Ute's belly, cleaning it in the snow before he tucked it into his waistband.

He waded around in the snow, searching for the pistol, still not finding it. He might never, and so he decided to look for something bigger and more important—the Ute's horse.

He would never make it to Leadville afoot, not with twenty men on his trail. The snow slanted down, dry, heavy flakes which washed out the day. Ruff was among the trees, trying to backtrack the Ute, but too much time had passed. His footprints were covered up.

He stopped, listening for the horse, but he heard nothing but the wind howl, the creaking of the tall pines. And then Mando Reyes burst from the trees, his horse frosted with ice, his eyes wild.

A rifle barked, and Ruff leaped behind a tree. Mando passed him, unable to stop his horse in that snow, and Ruff took off at a run.

He ran blindly through the trees, the wind and snow. The pounding of Mando's horse was close behind him, loud in his ears.

The snow was deep. The trees appeared out of the storm and the clouds an instant before Ruff reached them. Twice, he banged his shoulder against a tree. Each time he raced on, shrugging off the pain.

Mando was closer now, his rifle speaking loudly, singing promises of death.

Ruff was nearly past the rocky bluff before he saw it. He turned that way immediately and began clawing his way up the slope. The horse could not follow him, and there was a chance of escape that way—if Mando did not shoot him off the bluff.

Ruff didn't turn his head to look for Mando, he simply climbed. Climbed for all he was worth, scrambling over the rocks, banging his knees and elbows, tearing his fingers raw. His lungs were frozen, his limbs leaden. A bullet ricocheted off a rock inches from his hand and still he climbed. Another bullet ticked off his bootheel, but then he was up and over, lying flat on his back in the snow, his lungs afire, his heart hammering in his ribs.

Ruff dragged himself to his feet, pausing long enough to roll a rock down the bluff. He heard a horse whinny frantically, heard a bellowed curse, and then Ruff turned and stumbled on, holding his side as he ran into the high timber, as the snow tumbled down from out of a jumbled, rolling sky.

How far he ran he couldn't have said. Where he was he did not know. He only knew it was dark and cold and he was bone-weary. He found a tiny hollow between two snow-blanketed boulders, and there he sagged to the earth. There he would rest, there he would sleep. Let them come and kill him—he had to sleep.

The night wind rattled the pines and howled mockingly among the rocks. Ruff sat huddled in his hollow, his arms wrapped around his shoulders, his knees drawn up. It did no good—it was cold, bitterly cold, and he began to wonder seriously if he was going to get out of this alive.

His body ached, his mind was numbed with cold. His thoughts drifted, and he was not sure if he was awake or asleep. He must have been sleeping, had to be, for a woman appeared and she walked to him, curling up against him, her body warm, her hair scented and soft against his cheek. It had to be a dream, and so he held Soledad tightly to him and with her head on his shoulder, he slept.

Day dawned clear and cold. The snow glittered under a cloudless sky. Now it seemed Ruff was daydreaming, because she was still there.

He gently disentangled himself from Soledad, looking down at her too beautiful face, nearly childlike in sleep. It was difficult to keep in mind how young she was. Valenzuela had kept her preened and varnished, impeccably made up. Here, with her dark hair all atangle, with the softness of sleep on her features, she seemed very young indeed.

Soledad said Valenzuela had taken her when she was twelve years old. She had lived with him, she said, for nine years. That made her just twenty-one. She had seemed much more mature, but then they had been hard years.

She awakened now, and the look of innocence was lost. Her mouth firmed itself, her eyes flashed. Then she smiled. "Oh! I thought I was dreaming. I did find you."

"How?" Was there anyone else likely to find him?

"When you ran, I ran too. I wanted to be with you; it was my chance to get away from Ernesto. I rode frantically, I had no idea where I was. The others were chasing you and I fell in behind them.

"After the avalanche I lost you, but I kept riding. There were tracks in the snow and I thought they might be yours, but they were those of Mando Reyes.

"He didn't even see me. His eyes were savage. He rode hunched forward, all intent on his work. Then it occurred to me that he was following you and all I had to do was follow him. I don't know what had happened to the others by then. I suppose they were spread out across the mountain.

"It began to snow heavily again, and I lost Mando. I was growing desperate. My horse stepped in a hole—or maybe he stumbled over a root—and broke his leg."

"You don't have a horse?" Ruff interrupted. He had hoped . . .

"No. I had to come on afoot. Where I was going I don't know. I only knew I wasn't going back to Ernesto. The snow was swirling all around. I kept falling. I was terribly exhausted. Then I heard the shots.

"I crept to the edge of the bluff, very nearly tumbling over, and I saw Mando below me riding through the woods. Then, some time later, I saw you. You climbed the bluff and rolled a rock down—I think you broke his leg," she said, smiling with pleasure. "He was rolling around in the snow, clutching it.

"I saw you come up, but you ran on. So fast I could

not keep up. Then by luck I saw you, and here I am."
She spread her hands and smiled, presenting herself.

"I almost wish you hadn't found me," Ruff had to tell her. "It's going to be difficult enough."

"They'll never find you."

"They might. The storm's blown over."

"We can keep to the timber. With luck . . ." She stopped. Maybe it had occurred to her that Ruff Justice might have already used up all of his luck.

"You'll have to try to keep up, Soledad," he told her, taking her hands between his. Amazingly they were warm despite the biting cold. Her eyes were intent, searching. She nodded.

"I will. I'm strong," she insisted. "You'd be surprised how strong I am."

Ruff had a fleeting, vivid memory of those sturdy thighs, of the grasping, animal strength of her arms. He nodded.

"We've got to keep moving. If they catch us, they'll kill us."

"They'll never catch us," Soledad said brightly. "We'll outrun them. They don't know where the valley is, do they? And then we'll wait. If we have to wait all winter. Then we'll walk out in the spring, rich beyond . . . what's the matter?"

She cocked her head curiously at Ruff Justice, a bright smile on her perfect lips.

"Who told you about that valley, Soledad?"

"I overheard. The night you came to the hacienda. I was on the balcony, listening."

"And then you came to my room, asking me to take you away."

"Yes, but that had nothing to do with it!" She laughed.

"Is that why you begged Ernesto to bring you along—because of the treasure?" he asked.

"No!" Her denial was a strong one. She clung to him,

her fingers kneading his shoulders, her black eyes fixed on his. "It was because of you, darling."

"And it would make no difference if there was no treasure, no valley of golden tombs?"

"Of course not, darling!" She kissed his mouth.

Ruff took her hands and pried them free. "Good—because there isn't any such place, Soledad. It was all made up."

She took a half-step back awkwardly. Her mouth opened, hesitated, smiled. "You're joking, darling."

"I'm not."

"But I *heard* you, heard how you and your partner were running from the posse . . ."

"It never happened. I work for the United States Army, Soledad. It was all a scheme to lure your husband across the border so he could be hung."

"No." Her voice was muted. She shook her head and said savagely, "No! You're lying. I saw the ring."

"The ring was genuine. Eleven years ago an Indian trader got it from a Northern Ute. The Indian didn't know anything about where it came from, or if he did, he wouldn't talk. He was killed by some white men who tried to make him talk. The ring was the reality the entire fable was hooked on. But it was only that—a fable.

"I don't know what happened to the Fortunas. No one does."

"You bastard!" She had been standing, fists folded, her face draining of color. Now she shrieked. "You bastard!" she screamed again, and stood there, shaking, and it was with anger, not with the cold. She launched herself at Ruff, and he had to hold her wrists or have his eyes clawed out.

"He'll kill me," she sobbed. "Kill me!" She stepped back, holding her hands to her face.

Soledad had made a gamble and had lost. Whether or not Ernesto Valenzuela beat her—and Ruff tended to think that much was true—she had decided to try to get away from him, to latch onto Ruff Justice, who would make her rich and keep her comfortable. But she could not have known it was all a lie. Now she had deserted her husband, and Ruff knew it was as she said—if Valenzuela caught up with her now, he would kill her.

"All right." Ruff shook her by the shoulders. "We've both got to run for our lives. Forget the treasure, everything else. We've got to run to live. Do you understand?"

She nodded her head weakly and gave a little snuffle.

"With any luck we should be able to make Leadville. It can't be more than eight or ten miles off. We've got a lead on them, and if we stick to the timber and keep moving, we should be able to make it. You've got to do it, Soledad! Can you?"

She repeated her nod and snuffle.

"All right, then. Let's have at it."

The morning was cold, bright, and clear. Sunlight mirrored off the long snowfields and glittered in the icebound pines. It was all amazingly beautiful, and quite deadly.

They climbed the low, spruce-covered ridge behind them, and Ruff took his bearings, pausing to survey the land behind them, looking for any sign of pursuit, for smoke or a patch of color where none should have been, but he saw nothing. Nothing but the long ranks of pines, the gleaming snowfields, and above it all the haughty, towering Rockies.

Soledad's breathing had eased, and so Ruff nodded his head. He didn't intend to speak any more than was absolutely necessary. In this stillness sound carried incredible distances.

They reached the bottom of the spruce-clad hill and had to cross a small clearing, perhaps half a mile wide, where a creek twisted and gurgled across the snowy meadow.

Soledad stayed at his heels, making as good time

through the knee-deep snow as Ruff did. The divided riding skirt she wore didn't encumber her much, though Ruff doubted the fancy buttoned boots she wore were doing much to keep her feet dry.

Again they were into timber, and Ruff quit holding his breath. They moved through a vast forest of blue spruce and occasional cedar. Here not only were they screened from sight, but the snow was not so deep. Now and then the rising sun would melt the ice and snow which clung to the trees and a shovelful would fall to the earth. The first time it happened Soledad nearly jumped out of her skin.

It was unnerving, and as the sun warmed, it was more frequent. At times the plopping of falling snow sounded like pursuing footsteps.

It was cold among the pines, and Ruff shivered. He kept his knife—the one he had taken from the Ute—in his hand, though what good it would do against men armed with rifles he could not have said. Still it was something to grip, to offer some reassurance that he was not completely defenseless.

To stay within the forest they had to climb again, and the going was difficult. They were up high and the altitude was telling.

They paused briefly, halfway up a rocky slope, and Soledad clung to him, panting. It wasn't an embrace of any kind, she simply needed his support. She was a strong woman, but she had spent most of her recent life sitting on her haunches in Valenzuela's hacienda—it hadn't prepared her for a ten-mile trek through high-country snow.

"Let's go on," Ruff said. "I don't intend to be out here after nightfall."

"How far have we come?" she asked, still gasping for breath.

"Not far enough. Less than halfway. And the worst is yet to come."

There was timber downslope, but it was widely scattered—it looked as if someone had cleared it once, or maybe a forest fire had thinned the trees. But still they might make it, might make it easily. From atop the last ridge Ruff had caught sight of a thin tendril of smoke far in the distance and seen a greenish stain against the snow—it was a roof, and the smoke was rising from a chimney.

Now they hurried on, Soledad tripping and stumbling in the heavy snow. The wind had increased, and now it shoved at their backs, lifting their hair, chilling them. Ruff's mustache was frosted with frozen breath. His hands had no feeling in them.

"Look!" Soledad screamed and Ruff's head came around.

He could see them too, all too clearly. Horsemen a mile or so upslope, driving their horses through the deep snow, riding directly at them. It was Valenzuela and a dozen of his men—Ruff recognized the big black the bandit king rode even at that distance.

"Come on!" There was nothing for it but to turn, to run as far and as fast as they could. But it was useless. They weren't going to outdistance those horses, and they damn sure weren't going to outrace the bullets.

There was no choice but to stand there like a madman in the snow, waving his knife at a dozen armed men until they cut him down, and so they ran, trying for the deepest timber, which was none too heavy.

Soledad went down, and Ruff yanked her to her feet, cursing himself for getting tangled up with this woman. She was exhausted now, her face expressionless, with little more color than the snow.

Glancing over his shoulder, Ruff could see Valenzuela closing fast. The first bullet was cut loose by an overanxious vaquero, and it screamed into the woods over their heads.

They lurched into the trees, Ruff pulling Soledad along, trying to lose them in the tangle of dead vines and towering spruce, trying to find a place where the horses could not go.

It was too late for that. Valenzuela was into the woods now, not five hundred yards behind. Soledad went down again, and Ruff almost felt like leaving her there. But he didn't. He yanked her to her feet.

"I can't go on," she complained. "Leave me. Let him kill me, I don't care."

Ruff tucked his knife away, and, muttering curses, he shouldered the woman. Then he went on, moving at an awkward lope. The snow was deep and Soledad was heavy.

He rushed down a slope, slipping twice, going down hard once, and entered a ravine clotted with willow, blackthorn, and wild raspberry, all now dry and gray. Ruff fought his way through the thorny tangle, his face and hands torn by thorns and brambles, until he found a small clearing in the heart of the thicket. He put Soledad down.

"What are you doing?" she asked with utter weariness.

Ruff put his finger to her lips and motioned with his hands for her to stay there. He looked upslope; there was no sign yet of Valenzuela.

With a last glance back at Soledad, who watched him with miserable, uncomprehending eyes, Ruff ducked low and worked his way out of the thicket.

He ran along the creek bottom, the rush of white water loud in his ears. His tracks were clearly defined in the deep snow. He slowed for a minute, trying to gather his strength.

He heard the shout and broke into a trot. Across his shoulder he could see the vaqueros break from the timber, Valenzuela at their head. He saw Valenzuela's gun go up, heard the report, and he dipped into the hollow.

Here there was only willow brush growing along the quick-flowing freshet. Ruff crossed the creek in a long leap and continued to run, his long-legs carrying him swiftly down the canyon.

He passed a head-high boulder and continued on, the horsemen fording the creek behind him. Suddenly Ruff was in timber again, and he broke for the slopes. Circling back, his heart racing, he found the boulder he had passed.

He crawled out onto it, ducking low as Valenzuela's horse pounded past, kicking up rooster tails of snow. Ruff pressed himself against the cold stone, waiting. He wanted the last man.

When he saw him he leaped. With a running start off the rock he collided like an express train with the vaquero, and they slammed to the earth. The soldier was already going under, and Ruff helped him with a hard right hand chopped to the jaw.

It was Ignacio.

Ruff snatched his pistol and ammunition belt and sprinted after Ignacio's horse, which had gone dancing off through the trees.

With much coaxing and patience Ruff caught up the reins of the frightened, lathered roan. Now he was mounted, and had Ignacio's handgun and his Winchester.

"Justice!"

Ruff wheeled around sharply in time to see Ignacio stagger toward him. Ruff drew the Colt at his belt, but he didn't need it. Ignacio fell face downward into the snow, and Ruff saw the broken arrow in his neck.

A Ute broke from the woods, and then another. Ruff ducked behind the horse, fired two wild shots, and hit the saddle with a running mount, the war whoops ringing in his ears.

The Utes were afoot, and he put distance between himself and the Indians. Winding upslope, he got into heavier timber. Then he sat, letting the horse blow. The wind was hard off the north, and it cut through his clothing like icy prongs.

Now, dammit, he had to go back down there to get the woman. On the slope opposite him he could see Valenzuela's force. Four, five shots sounded rapidly, but they were not aimed at him.

Shadows sifted through the timber as the Utes stalked the Mexican force. Ruff heard a chilling, echoing scream, and he shivered, telling himself it was the wind which produced that reaction.

A man with any brains would have left Soledad down in that valley, figuring she was going to get what she deserved. Ruff thought of it; but he wasn't built that way. No woman deserved what the Utes would do to Soledad if they captured her.

Nor did any woman deserve the treatment Ernesto Valenzuela could dish out. He heeled the roan and dipped down into the valley where the battle raged.

... ...

12

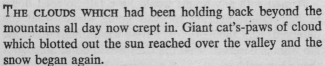

THE CLOUDS WHICH had been holding back beyond the
mountains all day now crept in. Giant cat's-paws of cloud
which blotted out the sun reached over the valley and the
snow began again.

It was both good and bad. They couldn't see Ruff so
easily through the storm, but neither could he see them,
and the Indians were masters at concealment.

It would be safer afoot, perhaps, but Ruff had no intention of letting go of the horse now that he had one. If he
had to run he would need the roan desperately.

Guns still popped along the ridge. It looked as if Valenzuela's men had dug in near the top of the hill. That
could be fatal.

Ruff had had more experience Indian fighting than
most anyone he could think of. Forting up was all right if
you had the supplies to do it, or expected relief. Out here
Valenzuela had neither. The Utes would take their time
and pick them off one by one.

All of that could work to Ruff's advantage. Valenzuela
was pinned down and the Utes had their eyes on the
Mexicans. He was halfway sure he could make it out of
there right now . . . but for the woman.

He tied the roan to a clump of brush, and with the rifle
in hand he worked his way down a rocky arroyo. The

snow was beginning to thicken now, and the wind whipped and snarled in the pines.

The wind covered the sounds he made as he moved, but that was little comfort. He kept his eyes moving, kept the rifle ready. He made the creek and worked his way into the brushy thicket there. Crouching low, he wove his way toward where he had left Soledad.

If only the woman hadn't disregarded his instructions—in that case it was probably too late for her. Soledad's only hope had been to stay put. If she hadn't moved . . .

She hadn't. Breaking through the screen of brush, Ruff saw her on the ground, her arm held protectively over her face. Hovering over her was a Ute brave.

He never saw Ruff coming. Justice was to him in five steps, his knife coming up from his belt. He caught the Ute's mouth with his left hand and drove the blade deeply into his back, angling up to catch the heart. The Ute went down without a struggle, and Ruff let go of his mouth. He would never cry out again.

Soledad came to Ruff on her knees, and she clung to his legs.

"I've never been so scared! God, what did I do to deserve this?"

She kept it up until Ruff had to slap her to silence her. Then he jerked her to her feet and, motioning for her to stay low, he began winding his way back toward the arroyo.

Up that, to the horse, and then over the ridge and to Leadville. If all went right.

It didn't.

Clambering up the rocky ravine through the snow, they entered the woods, exhausted from altitude and cold, their legs rubbery, their lungs filled with searing pain. Ruff went to where he had concealed the horse, finding the

133

spot easily. Someone else had found it easily too—the roan was gone.

There were two sets of moccasin tracks in the snow, and Ruff crouched down, listening, trying to hear any sound which did not belong above the howl and shriek of the wind.

Nothing. They were long gone, apparently. They had their booty. And Ruff had a long walk ahead of him. He returned to Soledad and dragged her to her feet.

"Where's the horse?"

"Gone. The Utes got it."

"What now?" she cried in exasperation. She was going to pieces out here. Some people aren't cut out for the wilderness. They have a certain raw toughness about them, but they haven't got what it takes for country like this. Soledad was one of them.

"What do you think?" Ruff growled. His voice was harsher than he intended, but he was feeling mad. "We walk out."

"I can't go another step."

"You can go another step, and then another, and another—or you can stay here and take your chances," he whispered savagely.

He started striding away through the pines, and when he looked back she was scurrying after him.

They worked their way up and over the pine ridge before them and plunged down the far slope through the whirling, thickening storm. The gunshots behind them were muffled now, far distant.

Suddenly Ruff grabbed Soledad's shoulder, and he yanked her behind a huge lightning-struck pine. They stood there breathlessly, Ruff's hand over Soledad's mouth, his body pressing hers to the tree. Her eyes were wide with anxiety.

Ruff could just make them out through the snow. Two men, white, riding eastward toward Leadville. They weren't dawdling, but they weren't racing their horses either. They seemed to be looking for something.

They weren't Valenzuela's men. The vaquero costumes they all wore were easily distinguishable. Who were they? Trappers or traders caught in the high-country storm, fleeing the Indians?

The sensible thing to do was to catch their attention and ride double into Leadville, but something within Ruff told him that it was not a good idea. They were gone, the screen of clouds closing to swallow them up, and Ruff let Soledad go.

"Who were they? Why didn't you stop them?" Soledad demanded.

Ruff simply shook his head. He led the way off down the hillside once more. They had to move slowly, and even then Ruff nearly led them into a hidden crevice. The snow was a mad, twisting howl. Ruff moved one leg and then the other, not thinking about how cold it was, that his legs were numb. His feet could have been miles away. His nose and ears seemed brittle enough to break off. But they plunged on.

When they could go no farther they cuddled together in a semi-protected hollow made by the root mass of a fallen pine. There, staring with red eyes at the blustering night storm, his muscles stiff and weary, Ruff passed the night restlessly.

Morning was clouded, but the snow had stopped.

He rose with difficulty, stretched his leg muscles, and then started to awaken Soledad when he heard it. A low moan, a whimpering, lost sound like that of a pup. Ruff moved into the low brush surrounding their hollow, his thumb drawing back the curved hammer of his Winchester.

He crouched low, listening for silent minutes before the sound came again. He crept that way, keeping his head below the brush.

He circled patiently, moving each foot with infinite care, making no more sound than a feather drifting on the wind.

The sound was so near that it startled him the next time. Ruff straightened up and eased behind the sheltering bulk of a woodpecker-pocked pine tree. Then, easing his head forward, he saw it, and his heart thumped twice. Then slowly, grimly, he smiled.

He moved to the injured man and crouched over him, searching him for weapons. He had none.

"Get up, Valenzuela."

The Mexican's eyes slowly opened. The whites were yellow, his focus slow in coming. He was pallid; his mouth was set into a crooked line. He looked old, much older than Ruff remembered.

"I'm dying," Valenzuela said.

"Where'd they hit you?"

Valenzuela jabbed a finger toward his leg. Setting the rifle aside and out of reach, Ruff slit the bandit leader's pants and had a look.

It was nasty. A bullet had torn away half the meat on the back of his thigh. But the artery had been missed, the bone was intact.

"I think you're going to make it," Ruff said.

"To be hung?" Valenzuela asked, attempting to smile—it came out more like a twisted grimace as pain interrupted the expression.

"Probably. I hope so."

"It was all a trick, wasn't it? I underestimated you, Justice. I thought you were a cheap crook, a fool too blind to see what you had found. I don't know when it came to me, but it did. I saw it in your eyes one day. We faced each other and I saw it. You were no fool. I couldn't turn back, though, I'd gone too far. Greed."

He fell silent, clamping his jaw tight as Ruff gently held the torn muscle in place and wound the tail of Va-

136

lenzuela's shirt around the leg to hold it in position. It wasn't much of a bandage, but the cold had slowed the bleeding, and with luck he would last until Leadville.

"Can you walk?"

"I made it this far."

"Try it."

"No sense in it, is there? I might as well stay here. But I'll try—hell, there's always a chance with a jury."

Valenzuela barely made it to his feet. He went white to the lips with the pain of it, but whatever else Valenzuela was, he was no coward. He hobbled forward to lean against the tree.

"Hold it. I'll cut you a branch to use for a cane."

That accomplished, they hobbled on. Ruff was really worried now. The girl had slowed him down enough, but now with Valenzuela, who was scarcely able to walk, they were reduced to a crawl.

"How many of your men are left?" Ruff asked.

"How many? I don't think any, although a few might have gotten away. If you're worried about them coming to rescue me, don't. They've sense enough to ride south and not toward Leadville—after all, I'm not worth a lot to them now. They'll return to the rancho, any who are alive, and split up whatever money I've got there. They know I'm through . . . I know it."

They broke out of the brush to confront Soledad Valenzuela.

She stood there motionlessly, her face utterly blank for a single moment before it twisted itself into a mask of rage and hate. She leaped at Valenzuela, hands clawing, and he was knocked down, Soledad climbing all over him, flailing at him with tiny fists.

"You bastard!" She screamed. "You rotten bastard, why won't you die! Miserable *cabrón,* filthy pig!"

Ruff pulled her off, screaming and kicking. He had to slap her and shake her.

"Stop it. Dammit, he's wounded."

"Kill him!"

"I won't kill him. He's my prisoner."

"He deserves to die," Soledad said. Her breast rose and fell with each breath. There was snow on her skirt and arms. Pine needles clung to her dark, unkempt hair.

"No one has ever debated that," Ruff said. Briefly he let a hand rest on Soledad's shoulder. "He deserves to die, but he'll go out legally."

"Maybe he will get away. Maybe the jury will let him off."

"Maybe."

"Ah!" She waved her arms in surrender. "Dammit all, do what you want!" She sat down on a snow-frosted rock, her face in her hands.

Ruff turned away briefly, looking ahead at the trail he meant to follow out of there. Briefly—it couldn't have been for more than a few seconds—and then it happened.

He heard Soledad shriek, heard the gun, and when he whirled back she was standing there laughing, the derringer smoking. Valenzuela was sagged against the snow, blood leaking from his skull where his right eye had been.

Ruff tore the pistol out of her hand and hurled it away. Soledad continued to laugh. She laughed until the tears ran from her eyes and were frozen against her cheeks.

Ruff stood up. There was no pulse. Valenzuela was dead and the game had ended suddenly.

"I was going to use that little gun on you," she said as if she could not stop herself from speaking. "I was going to wait until I could see the town and then I was going to put the barrel of that tiny gun to your skull, Ruff Justice. Then he came. He came and I could not stop myself. I hated him. Truly, deeply hated him for every moment of these last nine years."

She spun, her black eyes fiery. "And I'm glad I did it. Glad he is dead. Let him rot in hell. He was filth!" She walked to him and quite deliberately spat on the corpse of Ernesto Valenzuela.

Ruff watched her, watched the trembling of her shoulders, the glittering malice of her eyes, the sullen pout of her lips. Then he spoke.

"Let's get moving. That shot could be heard for miles."

Soledad followed meekly, and even when Ruff broke into a trot, she kept up with him. She was ghostlike now, as if she had lived only to hate, and now, her hating done, she was without spirit or purpose.

Ruff labored up the piny slope, and suddenly he could see the town. It was an ugly, gray collection of colorless buildings smeared over the slopes, but it was beautiful just then.

"Leadville," he said to himself, although Soledad was at his shoulder, gasping. Her eyes stared out at nothing. Ruff touched her shoulder. "Let's get on down there."

She simply went along, asking nothing.

It was a mile more until they found the old wagon road. It was deeply rutted and muddy beneath the snow, but it was the first sign of civilization they had seen in weeks. There was a road, and the end of that road was in Leadville; the end of the long, bloody trek which had begun all those months ago in Arizona.

"Come on."

Soledad only nodded. Where were her thoughts? She seemed far distant. Those beautiful black eyes were clouded. Ruff wondered if she had lost her mind.

They tramped eastward, the mud to their ankles. The wind was cutting off of the high slopes, the sky clouded and threatening.

Ruff could hear the sound of far-distant machinery— the ore crushers and stamp mills of Leadville. Once he thought he heard a human voice raised in a joyous whoop, but he couldn't be sure.

They were temporarily out of sight of Leadville. The

road looped around a small, cone-shaped, timbered hill. Ruff, relaxed now, moved with an easy, long stride.

When the two men came out of the woods he had no reason to expect trouble. Until the man on the sorrel horse aimed the big blue Colt at him, and Ruff, in that instant, recognized him.

"Harry H.!"

The man smiled back and cocked the hammer of the Colt.

13

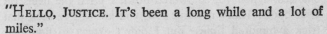

"Hello, Justice. It's been a long while and a lot of miles."

"Hello, Harry H." Ruff nodded to the other man. It was Yates, Harry's right-hand man at the prison.

"You want to drop that rifle," Harry asked, "or do I have to shoot you through the knee?"

Ruff dropped it, and Yates slipped from his horse, walking to Ruff Justice, slipping his belt gun from its holster.

"You got this wrong, Harry," Ruff said, hoisting his hands. "But it doesn't matter. Take me in."

Harry Hammerschmidt laughed. A long, braying laugh which shook his meaty shoulders.

"I thought you were clever, Justice. I really did. You disappoint me, boy."

"What are you talking about, Harry?"

"I think you know. You should have been a confidence man, Justice, you know that? You understand a hell of a lot more than you let on. You know why I'm here, don't you?"

"The ring?" Ruff guessed. "The ring is gone. It's in Mexico. How did you find it?"

"It was simple. I make my living by keeping my eyes and ears open, Justice—or I did. I've gambled it all on this. When a man checked into the prison I made it a point to learn all about him. Was he a bankrobber, a swindler? If he'd made a big haul, had they recovered the loot? If there was a profit to be made off the convicts, I knew. Me and Yates. Right, Yates?"

Yates nodded.

"But how did you get on to me?" Ruff wanted to know. He had his eyes on Harry's Colt. There was no chance of trying for it. There were two guns trained on them, and both men made a point of staying away from Ruff.

"How? It was simple!" Harry H. laughed. "I don't take chances. When you showered down I pried the heels off your boots. That's nothing new, you know. I've seen that trick a hundred times. But I didn't expect to find that ring. I was going to snatch it right then, but as it turns out, I'm glad I didn't. I knew something was up, and once you were locked up properly, I got a little digging done."

"And came up with the Fortuna treasure tale?" Ruff was weary now, weary with the long trek, with the fighting, with Harry H.

"That's right. A thing like that can't be kept a secret."

"No." Ruff shrugged. "You're right, Harry."

"I knew if you got out of the prison you'd make a break for the rest of it. Who wouldn't? Oh, not at first, maybe, but you'd go back for it."

"And so you followed me."

"I did. First I had to make sure you'd get out, didn't I?"

So it was Harry and not the warden who had left the gate open, kept the dogs in, provided the horses.

"You crossed me up going to Mexico, but I went along, me and Yates. You could have knocked me over with a feather when I saw who your pals were."

"Valenzuela?"

"Yes, Valenzuela, you fool! But it made a deal of sense. You knew this was Indian country, and you needed

142

an escort. You threw in with Valenzuela. It made it tougher on me. I couldn't see a way to get the treasure away from that army he had, but I had already gone too far to turn back, and so I stuck with you on the trail— and now it looks as if things are going to work out just fine."

Ruff's lips barely moved when he answered, "It's not going to work out at all, Harry."

"What do you mean? Are you saying you won't take me up there?"

"That's right."

"Not now. We'll cool our heels till the Utes drift away, till the snow stops. Hell, Justice, I'm as good as Valenzuela. We won't have so many ways to split now."

"No, Harry." Ruff was tired of explaining it. He was tired of greed, and sick to death of the killing this fable had produced. "You don't get it. There's no treasure up there! None at all."

"I won't swallow that."

"It's true."

"You must think I'm stupid!" Harry roared. He didn't believe Justice for a minute. He had to believe in the Fortuna treasure, had to believe Justice knew where it was. He had given up too much. "Listen, Justice, I'm desperate. I can't go back. There's things that happened on my backtrail, things they could lock me up for. I'm not going to play with you." He drew a bead, lining up his front sight with Ruff's head. "You can talk or you can die."

Ruff simply stared at him. He was boxed in again. He laughed out loud, and Harry H. just stared at him. Soledad stood apart, staring at nothing, the wind tossing her dark hair. Yates was scowling, but he looked uncomfortable.

"Sure, Harry," Ruff said, still laughing. "We're partners. You deserve it as much as Valenzuela did. We'll sit out the snows and then we'll go up there, and we'll hunt

143

for that valley of golden tombs. We'll hunt for it until we find it or die trying. Sure, whatever you say, you damned fool!"

Harry's face couldn't decide on an expression. He was furious and then amused, complacent and then worried. Had Justice gone mad up in those hills? What kind of thug was this Ruffin Justice, anyway? What was so damned funny?

"Where do you want to wait it out, Harry? Leadville? Out here? You got a cabin? How about Mexico or Denver?" Justice raved on. He must have taken a crack on the skull somewhere along the line. Harry H. and Yates exchanged a concerned glance.

"We'll find a place," Harry said slowly.

"Sure." Ruff laughed again. The damned lie would not die! If it was a tale of gold, you could tell them anything! Anything but the truth, that there was none. "Lead on, Harry, I'm all yours."

"We'll hole up out here for a while. I'll send Yates into town to pick up some supplies and see if he can get a line on a cabin."

Harry laid out his well-thought-out plans for Ruff, plans he had been mulling over for months. But Justice, damn him, he stood there grinning, nodding his head like a madman. Harry supposed the wilderness could do that to a man.

"You and the lady lead off walking. We'll be right behind you. When we find a good place we'll get off the road."

Ruff nodded, still grinning, and it unnerved Harry. But the tall man started off down the road, taking Soledad by the elbow to guide her, and Harry and Yates fell in behind them.

They rounded the bend in the road, and they were suddenly there. Forty blue-clad cavalry soldiers coming up the road toward them.

"Just keep your mouth shut, Justice," Harry whispered. "Remember, you've got as much to lose as I do. That gold. And don't forget, they'll lock you back up and add a term for escaping."

That said, Harry tucked his pistol away and held up his horse, smiling at the young lieutenant who rode at the head of the column.

"Morning, sir."

"Morning." The cavalry officer's eyebrows drew together as he studied the two men on horseback, the tattered, long-jointed man before them and the blank-eyed Spanish woman. "Have you seen anything of some renegade Utes?"

"Yeah," Harry said, removing his hat. "We ran into 'em. They're about five miles back east. Had 'em a little battle with some folks."

"Five miles, you say?"

"That's right, lieutenant. If you hurry, there's a chance you can round 'em up."

"Fine, thank you."

He turned to his sergeant and was ready to give the order to move out when Ruff Justice stepped forward and said, "Can you spare a patrol, sir?"

"A patrol?"

"More of an escort party, I suppose. These two men here are holding myself and this young lady prisoner."

"The hell you say! May I ask who you are?"

"The name's Ruffin T. Justice, sir. I'm an army scout detached from Fort Thomas on special duty for Major Harkness. The young lady is my prisoner."

Harry H.'s face fell three inches. He had counted on Ruff's greed and his fear of being thrown back in prison. An army scout! What in the hell had gone wrong?

"Can you prove any of that?" the lieutenant asked, staring now at Harry and Yates.

"If you get me to a telegraph key," Justice said.

A voice from the back of the ranks suddenly called out, "Justice! Is that really you, you old war horse? By God!"

A burly sergeant worked his way forward, and he was grinning.

"Danielson!" Ruff said, recognizing Scotch Danielson. The two men shook hands.

"Beg pardon, sir," Danielson said, "but I heard the name and thought I could clear things up."

"You know this man, sergeant?"

"I should smile. Me and Mr. Justice here fought a passel of Sioux together up in the Dakota Territory. Why, the stories I could tell . . ." he looked at Soledad Valenzuela and grinned. "By God, Mr. Justice, where *do* you find 'em?"

"You men, please drop your weapons and stand down to be searched," the lieutenant said to Harry H. and Yates. They did so, meekly, Harry wearing a stunned expression.

They gave up their weapons and surrendered, having no choice about it. But Ruff wondered if a moment's thought might not have changed that. He knew where Harry Hammerschmidt was headed—back into prison to live among the men he had beaten and mistreated.

Six cavalry troopers escorted Ruff and his prisoners into Leadville, and the gray, dingy town looked like home and Christmas.

The three prisoners were locked up by the town marshal. They went away without a protest. Harry still wore that stunned expression, and Soledad seemed not to know what was happening to her—she had left her awareness, her caring, up in those mountains.

Maybe in some confused way she had also loved the man she hated, the man she had killed. Ruff didn't know much about such things, and so he shrugged it aside, found himself a hotel room, and took a long, long bath.

He sent a telegram to Major Harkness at Fort Thomas,

giving the barest details, and then he found a restaurant where the steam from the kitchen kept the room warm while the wind howled outside, where the tempting smells of hot apple pie, coffee, and roast beef filled the room as a cute little freckle-faced waitress bustled around taking orders.

Ruff leaned back against the wall while he waited for his supper, and he let his eyes close halfway, let all of the tension of the long months past drain out of him. He was back among real people; it was over.

After eating he walked out onto the main street of Leadville. It was sundown; the mountains were deep in shadow, the stacked clouds rose high into the sky.

There were wild, beautiful columns of clouds, and the wind had carved hollows in them, and the sundown skies, golden with the last light of day gilded them, and there, stacked dreamlike against the deep blue of the sky, the clouds formed fantasies, and just for a moment, as the last brilliant, golden rays of the dying sun spattered them with color, they looked for all the world like a vast and beautiful valley of golden tombs.

14

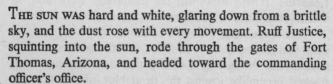

THE SUN WAS hard and white, glaring down from a brittle sky, and the dust rose with every movement. Ruff Justice, squinting into the sun, rode through the gates of Fort Thomas, Arizona, and headed toward the commanding officer's office.

He was kept waiting only a minute as the burly first sergeant went in and announced him, and then Major Harkness, his deeply tanned face both overjoyed and slightly sheepish, appeared.

"Ruff!" Harkness said it nearly as if it were impossible. His hand was thrust out, and Justice took it warmly. "Back from the dead. It's incredible!" The major opened his office door and led Ruff inside. He poured himself a drink and perched on the edge of the desk.

"I owe you an apology, Ruff."

"No. But an explanation would help," Ruff replied. "What went wrong?"

"What didn't?" Harkness said ruefully. He tossed down his drink.

Ruff Justice leaned back in the comfortable leather chair and crossed his long legs, placing his hat on his knee as Harkness poured himself another whisky.

"We were all poised here, as you know," Harkness explained. "We had our network of watchers along the border, and as soon as word came that you had lured Valenzuela back across the border, we would have been ready to close in.

"But!" Harkness gestured in exasperation. "The telegram we got from the state prison cut all of that off short. The plan was aborted."

"What did it say, exactly?" Ruff inquired.

"It said simply that Ruffin T. Justice had been murdered by the prisoner Mando Reyes. I felt like hell, knowing that I had caused your death."

"Who signed the telegram?" Ruff wanted to know. "Warden Donovan?"

"No. And there's some odd business there. Apparently both Donovan and his assistant, Forbes, resigned and then immediately disappeared. The new warden, a fellow named . . ." Harkness looked at the paper on his desk. "Harry Hammerschmidt, that's it. He sent the wire, with deep regrets and all."

"Good old Harry H." Ruff explained briefly about Harry and his part in all of this. "He made a profit out of every prisoner in that penitentiary, a good living. And then he saw a chance to make a big killing. He found the ring and got on to the plan—probably he or his spies overheard me telling Mando about my plans to escape."

"Good God!" Harkness looked more sheepish than ever. "And I was fooled by him. The message seemed official, though." He was thoughtful. "What about Warden Donovan? Where do you think he could have gone?"

"No telling," Ruff answered, recrossing his legs, "but if I were you, I might suggest to the authorities in Tucson that they have a look in the punishment cells at the state prison."

"Christ, yes!" Harkness leaped off his desk. "Where else would Hammerschmidt stash someone?" He walked quickly to the orderly room and told the first sergeant to get that message to Tucson as quickly as possible.

Ruff was smiling when he came back, and Harkness shook his head, "I must be getting old, Ruff. Damn, I feel like a fool."

"It doesn't matter now, sir. It's all worked out."

"Yes. Yes, it has, hasn't it?" Harkness allowed himself a small smile. "I've been after that bloody bastard Valenzuela for years, Ruff. You can't imagine how it's plagued my mind. Knowing he was sitting down there comfortably in Mexico where I couldn't get at him while my family lay cold and buried.

"But he's dead. You're sure?"

"Positive, sir. I was standing over him when he died," Ruff assured him. The major's smile deepened into one of satisfaction.

"Can you tell me about it? How it happened. The wire just said he was dead."

Ruff told him, taking the story all the way back to Mexico, to Soledad's abduction and her forced marriage. When he was through, with Soledad standing over the dead Ernesto Valenzuela in the snow, he saw Major Harkness give an involuntary shudder.

"A grim tale, Ruff. Most grim. One wonders what was going on in the woman's mind."

"There's no telling."

"And you think she's insane now?" Harkness asked.

"She is. After all, what was there left to hold her life together? She lived only to hate."

"Yes." Harkness nodded thoughtfully, and then sighed. "Well, we're going to have to spend a couple of days wading through the paperwork, Ruff. The report will be a dilly. After that, I suppose you've got some time off coming to you. Any thoughts on what you're going to do?"

"I have some strong thoughts on it," Ruff answered. "There's a dark-eyed lady in Sonoita I mean to look up. We were sort of abruptly separated last time."

"The one you were with when you were arrested."

"Uh-huh. I feel I kind of owe her an apology," Ruff said without a smile.

"You deserve it," Harkness said. "But I would have thought you'd had enough of these Spanish beauties after the last one."

"Maybe. But you know, old Bill Collins once stepped out of the barracks, threw back his arms, and took a good deep breath and sucked a bee right up his nose. Bill was a little more cautious after that, maybe, but he damn sure didn't give up breathing."

Sonoita was still there. Life went on as usual in the squat dusty adobe town. Chickens wandered the streets, and dogs lay flat on their sides, tongues dangling, in the shade of the cantina awning. A barefoot peon kid drove a donkey homeward.

Elena Cruz was still there.

When Ruff rode up she was pinning up her laundry. Her mouth was filled with clothespins. Her wash fluttered in the gusting dry breeze off the desert which dried her laundry almost before she had finished pinning it all up.

Ruff sat the glossy black horse he had picked up at Fort Thomas, and he watched her, liking the deft movements of her hands, the supple strength of her shoulders. She hummed a little tune as she worked. A strand of raven-black hair had fallen loose, and it curled past her small ear and wound down her coppery neck.

She must have felt his eyes on her. She whirled, her eyes briefly challenging. And then they softened, became welcoming beacons.

"Ruff Justice," she said with her deep accent, rolling the name off her tongue. "*Ai, bandito,* and so you have come back to Elena."

"Back to Elena." Ruff nodded.

"And the trouble? It is all over?"

"All over, Elena."

"Bueno." She dropped her handful of clothespins into the basket at her feet and walked to where he sat his impatient horse. Her skirt was striped gaudily, and it pressed against her thighs as she moved toward him. Her blouse was white, down off one shoulder, revealing a splendid golden-brown bit of female flesh.

"So why you sit your horse like that, hombre?" Elena smiled, a strong, white, Indian smile, and her hand rested on his thigh, the ends of her fingers crimping slightly, stroking him. "You going to run away, or you like to sit out in the sun all day, my tall man?"

"I was waiting for an invitation," Ruff said.

She stuck her toes into the stirrup on the offside, climbed up, and threw her arms around Ruff Justice's shoulders, dragging his head down to meet her full, lazy, devouring kiss.

"So now you got an invitation, Ruff Justice. Now you get down, get rid of the damn horse, eh?"

And he did so.

They drowsed in her bed. Elena lay sprawled, exhausted with their lovemaking, her long legs stretched out, her hair in a black tangle across the pillows.

Ruff ran his hand down her straight, slim back and up the astonishing curve of her buttocks. He bent his head and kissed her back, at the very tip of the tailbone, and he felt her quiver and murmur with pleasure.

He was naked and relaxed; the room was still warm with their efforts. Ruff moved closer to her, throwing his leg across her hips, letting his hand move between her thighs. She accommodated him by spreading her legs a little more, and he cupped her warmth in his palm, feeling content, feeling in some way that it had all been worth it—the mad chase over the mountains, the long, blood-soaked miles, just to return and press his hungry flesh against hers, to feel the soft pulsing of her body, to place his cheek against the soft swell of her ample breasts and

152

listen to her heart thudding as the day passed in lazy ease.

"This time you better stay for a while, Ruff Justice," Elena muttered into her pillow.

"This time I will stay for a while, Elena Cruz," he answered, kissing her shoulder and then her neck. His hand began gentle, stimulating motions.

"Ai, hombre," Elena breathed. "You want again? You make me exhausted."

All the same she rolled over, and she was smiling, her long tawny arms stretching out to him. Ruff bent his lips to hers, and as they kissed her hand dropped to his crotch, and she found him ready, swollen with eagerness.

"I am so hungry," Elena yawned as she tugged him to her, as her legs opened for him and she settled him in place with a short thrust of her competent hips.

"Me too."

Ruff entered her slowly, filling her as he watched her face, watched her eyes glow, her mouth go slack.

"In a little while," he told her, "we'll go out and I'll buy you a steak."

"And I think some wine, Justice. I think I would like some wine. Too much, maybe."

"All right. Wine too, too much wine, and we'll sit and talk until it is very late."

Her hips rolled against him as they talked and her hands clutched at his shoulders. "Then we will walk under the stars, eh, Ruff Justice?"

"Of course. We'll walk out onto the desert while it's still and cool. And then we'll swim in the river while the moon rises. We'll watch it for a long while and swim until we're exhausted."

"And then," she panted, "we will come back and sleep for days." She murmured a small sound as Ruff's efforts began to lift her to a crest of sensation. Her pelvis lifted and drove against his. Her breath came in short, labored gasps.

"For days . . ." he found himself unable to hold back, and he knew that Elena too was striving toward a sudden explosively hard climax, and he let himself go, feeling her tremble, feeling her sway and pitch, arch her back, and clutch at him until she abruptly found it and she fell back, stroking his shoulders, his thighs, her breath soft against his ear as he murmured tiny endearments in Spanish, in English, in the nonsensical language of love.

"I shall have to sleep for days," she said from out of her drowse.

Her body was still bathed in a warm golden glow, and Ruff clung to her, kissing her throat, her breasts, her ears, prolonging it. They lay together, their bodies exhausted, utterly satisfied, utterly at peace, clinging together in the soft darkness.

The door slammed open behind them, the latch splintering off, and he came slowly forward from out of the night, dragging a leg as he moved heavily toward the bed where Ruff Justice lay.

His breathing was deep, ragged, and tight. The faint light from the stars illuminated his dark, broad face, and Ruff Justice sprang from the bed, hitting the floor as Mando Reyes lifted his Colt and fired three times in rapid succession.

Elena screamed and darted toward the far corner of the room.

"Justice! Come out, you bastard!"

Ruff had rolled under the bed, and Reyes fired twice more, the mattress jumping as the bullets hit it. The gunshots echoed loudly in the tiny room, and smoke filled the house as Mando fired again.

His gun was empty, but Reyes didn't care. He was beyond reasoning. His mind, always balanced dangerously, had snapped completely and he was not human any longer. He was a rogue grizzly, striking out at everything. And now he had cornered the hunter who had wounded him.

"You lied to me all along. You bastard! You broke my leg. Do you know what it was like, crawling out of those mountains? The Utes were all around, and it was snowing. It was cold and my leg was shattered. I always knew I would kill you, and now I have come to do it."

As he spoke he crossed the room, throwing a chair aside, kicking over a wooden table. He had his knife in his hand. His eyes were darkly gleaming, his mouth split into an ugly grin.

"Come out, Justice. Come out! I fix you maybe so you don't be with no woman ever. Leave you maybe, then come back and kill you slowly. Come out from under the damn bed, hombre!"

Ruff lay on his back beneath the bed. The floor was cold and hard. He could see Mando's boots as the big man slowly approached, dragging his crooked leg behind him. He could hear Mando's roaring commands, his raving threats, but he held himself still, not answering.

Ruff's gunbelt was in the far corner, impossibly distant. Mando was armed and bull-strong. He had the strength of madness in him.

Ruff glanced quickly toward the far corner. He could see Elena, naked and shivering, crouched in the corner, her eyes wide.

Mando's boots were only a stride away from the edge of the bed. The big man continued to mutter threats.

"I will kill you. First I will cut your fingers off. Then your balls, hombre. I'll leave you looking like butchershop scraps. Can you hear me?" His voice was a thundering boom. He threw his head back and howled. It was a chilling sound, not human at all. "Are you dead, Justice? Don't die so easily, *amigo*."

Ruff didn't intend to. Mando took another step, and Ruff's hand shot out to grab Mando Reyes' boot. He yanked hard, and Mando toppled over backward. Before he had hit the ground, Justice was rolling. He rolled out the far side of the bed as Mando, enraged, dove beneath the bed. Ruff leaped across the bed as Mando went under. He dove toward his gun in the far corner.

Before he could reach it, Mando, quick as a panther, had dragged him down by the heels.

Reyes was all over him now, panting, slavering. The knife went up, flashing silver in the vague starlight which shone into the room through the broken door.

The knife drove down at Ruff's chest, but Justice managed to grip Mando's forearm. The man was incredibly strong, however, and he only slowed the knife. He could not stop its descent. Mando was grinning, his eyes bulging as he put a hand to Ruff's throat, as he drove the knife inexorably downward.

Ruff heard the quick, light footsteps, saw the chair slam down against Mando's back, saw the blazing anger on the face of Elena Cruz.

Elena swung the chair against Mando's broad back, and he rolled aside in agony. He got to his feet and tossed her aside with a swipe of his massive arm. She banged against the wall and slid down it, sagging against the floor.

Justice was up now, and as Mando briefly turned his attention to Elena, Ruff hit him. He slammed a right hand to Mando's neck, saw the big man stagger slightly, and then, moving quickly, with desperate strength, Ruff managed to get hold of Mando's right wrist.

He yanked the knife hand up and back, twisting Mando's fist up between his shoulder blades. Then Justice bent the man's wrist double, and with a yowl of pain Reyes opened his hand and the knife clattered free.

Ruff kicked it aside and lifted a knee, driving it into Mando's kidney. Mando simply shrugged it off. Going low and straightening his arm, Mando came out of the hammerlock.

He kicked out against Ruff's bare knee and then

stamped down hard on Justice's instep. The pain was excruciating, and Ruff had to fall back. Elena hadn't moved yet, and Mando had Ruff cut off from his gunbelt.

Mando moved in and Ruff stepped back, moving in a circle. He threw the chair in front of Reyes and kicked over the table. Mando threw them aside and closed in.

Reyes was panting heavily, hunched slightly forward, his big fists balled. Ruff suddenly stopped and, moving in, slammed two hard, straight lefts to Mando's nose. The big man didn't even slow down.

With a bellow he lunged at Justice, getting his bearlike arms around Ruff's chest. He lifted Ruff from the ground and applied the pressure.

Those arms were like iron bands constricting around Ruff's ribcage, and Justice knew if he let it go on too long he was in trouble. He didn't let it go on.

He smashed the heel of his hand against Mando's nose, trying to break the bone and drive it up. At the same time he brought a knee up hard to Mando's groin.

His hand brought a stream of hot blood but had little other effect. The knee was dead center, and Mando dropped Ruff, falling back, gasping for breath, his gut heaving with the pain.

Ruff didn't let him get set; he bored in, winging three right-hand shots to Mando's face. He heard jawbone break under the third hook, and Mando's face altered into an anguished, utterly astonished mask.

But Reyes was not through yet. He roared and charged Ruff Justice, but there was no finesse to it. It was the charge of a bull, of an enraged wild thing, and Ruff was able to step aside and duck the mauling, savage attack.

Mando tripped and plunged forward into the wall. Ruff's breath caught. Mando, trying to regain his balance, placed his hand on the chair where Ruff's gunbelt hung.

The big man started forward, checked himself, and

slowly smiled. It was a terrible smile. Blood leaked from his shattered nose. His broken jaw hung loosely, giving his face a slack, subhuman expression. But the black, savage eyes were gleaming. Mando reached down and yanked Ruff's Colt from its holster.

Ruff dove for the floor as Mando raised the gun to waist level. Ruff's hand brushed something hard and metallic, and without thinking, he knew what it was and how to use it.

Ruff's hand closed around the haft of Mando's knife as the gun came up, and as the first shot from the .44 exploded over Ruff's shoulder, Justice drove up with the gleaming, deadly blade of the bowie.

It went deep into Reyes' body, just at the V where the ribs came together in the center of the outlaw's chest. Ruff came to his feet, twisting the blade, angling it up toward the Mexican's heart.

Mando still had the pistol in his hand, and as Ruff drove him against the wall, he tried to bring up the muzzle, but Ruff had struck the heart, and the blood flowed from the jagged, terrible wound in Mando Reyes' chest.

They were pressed together, Mando's horrible, shattered face next to Ruff's. His eyes still glittered with savage hatred, but he no longer had the strength to lift the Colt, no longer had the ability to squeeze that trigger.

His mouth opened and a gurgled, bloody curse frothed from his lips.

It was the last sound Mando Reyes was ever to make on this earth. He sagged downward, slipping down the wall, his blood pooling on the floor of the little adobe. And still Ruff Justice worked his knife, digging it deeper, twisting it, until Reyes was on the floor, his black eyes oddly peaceful, the Colt lying inert in his dead white hand, the warm blood puddled around him.

Then Justice let go. He staggered backward and hurled the knife angrily aside.

For a moment he stood over Mando, watching him, feeling his own heart pounding wildly, feeling the blood of his adversary against his own flesh.

Then he walked to where the woman sat limply against the floor and crouched down to sit beside her and hold her in his arms, feeling the warmth, the life of her.

She was crying, but soon she stopped, wiping her eyes. Her fingers touched Ruff's lips, and she kissed his naked chest.

"You told me there was no more of this," she said with a sobbing laugh.

"I'm sorry you had to be here. Sorry." He kissed her lips, tasting the salt of her tears. He held her tightly, saying nothing for a long while.

He felt her shoulder shrug, felt Elena take a deep slow breath. Then she pushed him back. "Help me up, Ruff Justice."

He did so. "Do you want me to go, Elena Cruz?" he asked, holding her close to him. "This was a terrible thing to see."

"Terrible. He was a madman, a madman." She turned then and looked toward the dead, crumpled form of Mando Reyes. "But I do not let such men ruin my life, eh?" she said, straightening herself, looking into the eyes of Ruff Justice.

"We do not let such men destroy our world, Ruff Justice. I will not have my evening ruined. It was a terrible thing, and I am sorry it happened. But," she said, "I am glad he is dead."

She moved nearer, and her breasts were warm against Ruff Justice. He stroked her fine, dark hair and held her as she trembled.

"We will go to the sheriff, Ruff Justice, and tell him about this. Then we will go and have our dinner and

Elena Cruz will drink too much wine. We will swim in the dark river until the moon rises and then we shall walk back from the desert and we shall sleep for days."

And they did.

WESTWARD HO!

The following is the opening section from the
next novel in the gun-blazing, action-packed new
Ruff Justice series from Signet:

RUFF JUSTICE #6: THE SPIRIT WOMAN WAR

1

•••• —————◆————— ••••

Fort Abraham Lincoln, Dakota Territory, 1878

THE WIND WAS hard off the north, bending the long
grass out of the plains. Sergeant Ray Hardistein stood before the orderly room squinting into the sun. It wasn't
quite right—it couldn't be, shouldn't be. He grinned suddenly and slapped his palm on his thigh, swinging open
the orderly-room door to holler to Pierce.

"Come out here, Sarge!" Hardistein called.

The first sergeant looked up with barely controlled impatience. A bulky, lethargic man, it was an ordeal as well
as an inconvenience for him to rise from his desk.

"What in hell for!"

Hardistein didn't answer. He simply waved a hand en-
thusiastically, and First Sergeant Mack Pierce, with a
heavy sigh, planted his palms on the desk top and heaved,
bringing his massive form to its feet.

Putting on his faded cap, he ambled to the boardwalk
in front of the orderly room. Hardistein was leaning
against the hitch rail, looking out toward the dead grass
plains beyond the stockade.

"What in hell is this, Ray?" Pierce asked. In answer
Hardistein just nodded, and Pierce's narrowing eyes lifted

to the road beyond the main gate. Then he too saw the horseman coming in.

Long, lean, clad in buckskins, astride a white-maned palomino, red plume thrust into his hatband, carrying a rifle across the saddlebows . . . "Can't be," Pierce said in a dry voice.

"Has to be," Hardistein said, glancing at the top sergeant. "Can't be anyone else, can it?"

"Holy Christ!" Pierce's curse was whispered. "Better tell Frank Howler and let him out the back gate. I'll warn the C.O."—Hardistein had already started toward the enlisted barracks—"and hide the women," Pierce added belatedly. Hardistein, already off at a dead run, never heard him. "Jesus!"

Pierce stepped down to the parade ground and stood watching. The in-rider's face took on definition, and now Pierce could see the long dark hair curling past the man's shoulders, see the flowing black mustache. "Jesus," he muttered again. Then he turned and went through the orderly room into the C.O.'s office without bothering to knock.

First Lieutenant Christopher Fairchild was sitting beside the C.O.'s desk, his eyes glazed, a month-old Denver newspaper on his lap. Fairchild looked up and yawned at the massive first sergeant.

"Where's the colonel?" Pierce demanded, all military etiquette briefly out the window.

"What . . . ?" Fairchild was torn between anger and curiosity. "What is it, Pierce?"

"Colonel MacEnroe, for God's sake, Lieutenant, where is he?"

"What is it? Cheyenne or Sioux?"

"Neither. It's worse than both of 'em, sir. Please, where's the colonel?"

"He returned to his quarters, said he had to—" Pierce

had already turned and was on his way out the door. "Pierce! Sergeant Pierce!"

The door banged shut. Christopher Fairchild, mentally preparing his speech on the lax discipline on the plains, snatched up his hat and followed. By the time he reached the front door things seemed to have come to a head.

What exactly was going on, Fairchild could not have said, but *something* sure in hell was.

Pierce was waddling across parade toward the enlisted barracks. From the sutler's store a dozen men, most with beer bottles in their hands, had appeared to clog the boardwalk. Another half-dozen men were running toward the gate from the grub hall.

Inside the barracks, out of Fairchild's puzzled view, Ray Hardistein was frantically trying to help Corporal Frank Howler into his boots and tunic.

"Damnit, Howler, get moving, can't you!"

It was a cry of anxiety not of urging. Howler was already moving as fast as a man could be expected to. One suspender was on, one off. His fly was open. Roused from a dream after a night's sentry duty, faced with sudden, impending doom, he was still clumsy with sleep, and his wild attempts to hurry simply tangled Hardistein's efforts.

"I'm moving it. I'm moving it, Sarge," Frank Howler said almost tearfully. He was a big, hulking man with a yellow, untrimmed mustache. Just now his eyes were red-rimmed, his face unshaven.

Hardistein tried to pull his tunic on him as Howler crow-hopped toward the door, one boot on, one partly on. At that moment Pierce burst in the door.

"God, are you still here!"

The two noncommissioned officers exchanged a worried glance. Through the open door of the barracks Howler could see the gathering men, see the dust and the pale horse, and he muttered a weak, "Oh, God!"

"Come on, come on!" Pierce grumbled. "I ought to just let him have you. It's your own damned fault, Howler."

"I never thought—hell, she was just a woman."

Pierce propelled Howler, who was nearly as big as he was, through the door, watching Howler's face turn again toward the gate, watching anguish pass across it. "Jesus—he's seen me!"

And he had. Pierce turned, watched as the tall man on the palomino tossed his rifle to a nearby soldier and kneed the horse forward at a dead run. A cheer went up and the soldiers at the gate started after the horseman, not wanting to miss it.

Howler tore himself out of Pierce's grip and ran toward the river gate. He was a bear of a man, heavy in the hips and shoulders, and Pierce would never have believed he could run that fast, but he was running now, arms pumping up and down, legs churning up the dust.

Hardistein sagged to the boardwalk, removing his hat. "Jesus! What now?" The horseman was nearly to them, his black hair flowing out behind him as he guided his well-trained horse with just the pressure of his knees like an Indian on a good buffalo pony.

"Get the Officer of the Day. Get me twelve good men," Pierce sighed.

"Twelve men who'll help break *this* up?"

"It's an order. Make it an order."

"It'll have to be," Hardistein said, rising, planting his hat, sprinting back toward the orderly room as Pierce, muttering profuse curses, ambled after the horseman.

Frank Howler was panting like a bellows. Looking across his shoulder, he could see the tall man on the palomino not thirty feet behind him. Howler tripped, thought he would go down, and miraculously recovered his balance by waving his heavy arms furiously.

He cursed the tall man, the army, and the woman who had started all of this.

There was no way he was going to outrun the man on horseback. Howler swung into the open door of the blacksmith's shop and stumbled through the cluttered smithy. He took three paces, still looking across his shoulder, before he stepped into the water bucket. Howler went down in a heap and Walters, the shriveled blacksmith, turned, holding a horseshoe in his tongs.

"What in hell is going on! Howler?"

Walters threw the horseshoe down and started forward angrily, but Howler was already on his feet, staggering forward. He looked back and yowled. Walters, looking toward the door himself, saw the man on horseback come through the doorway, ducking to clear the lintel.

"I'll be damned!" Walters said. He grinned and stood, hands on hips, watching.

Howler, his mouth opened as he gasped for breath, was heading for the back door of the smithy. He stopped long enough to throw a saddle onto the ground behind him and kick over a keg of nails. Neither held the pursuing horseman up for a second. The palomino nimbly picked its way through the litter, and the rider was only paces behind Howler as he went out the back door.

Walters' head swung back as he heard the cheers of the crowd. Two dozen soldiers, laughing, shouting, were following Howler and his tormentor. Pierce was waving an arm, urging them on, and it seemed they were in pursuit of the tall man, but it wasn't what you could call swift pursuit. It was a carnival parade.

Pierce's bellowing did nothing to speed the troopers. Walters lifted a finger toward the back door, watched as the soldiers passed by—some of them, failing to notice the spilled horseshoe nails, paying the price. Walters shook his head and followed them, wiping his hands on his leather apron.

Howler had burst from the smithy and was now fighting his way through the horses in the paddock. The animals milled excitedly, one rearing up as Frank Howler shoved them aside and, panting, made the gate. He opened it just as the man on the palomino entered the paddock from the far side. Howler rushed on.

He neglected to close the gate, and three dozen army bays trotted after him and onto the parade ground.

Lieutenant Christopher Fairchild, having seen the soldiers go into the blacksmith shop, had just decided to head that way himself when he saw Frank Howler, half dressed, half shaven, half mad, come running across parade. Behind him a herd of loose horses rounded the corner from the paddock, their hoofs thundering across the earth. Behind the horses came the lone rider on the palomino, his pace unhurried, his face immobile.

A dozen pursuing soldiers came next. Half of them seemed to be hopping along, favoring one leg or the other.

Fairchild stepped off the plank walk and shouted, "Howler, I order you to—"

Whatever he was going to order Howler to do was lost in the stampede of horses, the shouts of men. Howler was already past the lieutenant and making for the grub hall.

"You!" Fairchild leveled a finger at the man on the palomino. *What was his name?* Fairchild hadn't been at Fort Lincoln when this all started. The pointing finger didn't slow the horseman down; he seemed not even to see Fairchild. His blue eyes were intent upon his prey.

Fairchild spun around, saw Howler try to leap the watering trough, fail, send up a waterspout as he landed belly first in it. Then Howler was up, ducking under the hitch rail, clearing the boardwalk in two water-logged leaps as he crashed into the grub hall door.

Sergeant Ty Quinlan, the company cook, turned from his buffalo stew to see the huge form of Frank Howler burst into his kitchen, shove pots and pans aside, spill a fifty-pound sack of flour behind him, and rush through the room.

"Howler! You bastard! What in hell are you trying to . . . ?" Howler was already gone. Quinlan, wooden spoon still in hand, started after him, kicking his way through the jumble of pots and pans, sending up clouds of flour. Suddenly there was a roar behind him and Quinlan spun to see the man on the palomino riding through his dining room, scattering men. If that wasn't bad enough, on his heels came a dozen hopping, shouting soldiers. A table went over, and then another. Dishes clattered to the floor, and those men who were trying to eat began throwing their silverware at the mob rushing through the grub hall.

Food was flying everywhere now, and a half-dozen fist fights had started up, men tumbling over tables, destroying what was left of order.

Quinlan had to throw himself back against the wall as the palomino horse trotted unconcernedly through his kitchen, its flank banging more utensils from the wall, its hoofs throwing up a dense white floury fog.

Quinlan stood in the center of the cloud of flour, wiping his eyes. First Sergeant Pierce, huffing and red-faced, rushed past, and Quinlan grabbed his arm.

"Was that . . . ?"

"It was!" Pierce shouted, tearing his arm away from the cook.

"I'll be damned," Quinlan whispered. Then, throwing his spoon away, he joined in the mad pursuit which now counted two dozen men, a cook, three cook's helpers, a blacksmith, and—dead last—a raging first lieutenant.

Howler stumbled, went facedown, rose again, and staggered on. The sutler's door was open and that was his goal. He almost made it.

But the tall man, hard on his trail, kicked the palomino into a run and leaped from the saddle, colliding with Howler as he reached the plank walk.

Howler felt the weight of the man as he slammed into his ribs, taking him to the ground. Howler fought back with the fury of the panicked.

He had great strength in his arms, and he managed to take the tall man by the shoulders and roll him aside as he came to his feet.

But he was too slow. A sharp jab caught his cheek as he stood, splitting the flesh, and blood trickled down Howler's face into his mouth.

He staggered backward, his back meeting the wall of the sutler's store. "For God's sake," he sputtered, "she was only an Indian squaw, I didn't know!"

He might as well have been talking to the moon. The tall man's fists flashed before his eyes, and Howler felt his head snap back and collide with the wall. The stars flickered on behind his eyes and he covered up with his forearms, ducking low to evade the knifelike thrusts of the tall man's fists.

They were razors slashing at his face, hammers pummeling his ribs. Howler moved along the wall, his forearms crossed in front of his face.

It may have been anger or humiliation—now he could hear the hooting of the troopers, the catcalls. It may have been sheer animal pride, but Howler suddenly stopped, tired of backing away from the tall man in buckskins.

With a bellow of anger he went to the attack, moving in heavily, flat-footed, hooking trip-hammer rights and lefts to the ribs of his tormentor. The tall man laughed! Laughed! And Howler felt his courage begin to sink.

A left clubbed the right side of his skull, and as he lifted an arm to defend against it, the second left dug into his liver.

Howler backed away again, firing out furiously with hard punches. Already his weighty arms were tired, however; already the tall man had him reeling.

A fist glanced off his temple, a second dug into his

wind, and Howler let out a low grunt, doubling up, only to meet a vicious uppercut which caught him on the point of the chin.

Howler whirled and backed away. He was inside the sutler's store suddenly, and he threw barrels of lard, and cases of canned goods to the floor as he backed away. The sutler was whining loudly, pulling his hair as Howler destroyed the store, as the tall man placidly, methodically, closed in on him.

Howler threw a saddle at the tall man, kicked out savagely, and, panting, tipped over the pickel barrel. He found the beer bottles and had hefted one when the sutler cried out pleadingly, "Not the beer! God, not the beer!"

Howler threw the bottle anyway; the buckskin-clad man simply ducked and came in, fists flying. One landed flush on Howler's eye and he staggered back, kicking out savagely, uselessly. He swiped at the tall man with an ax handle, had it yanked out of his hands as if he were a child, felt the stunning impact of a perfectly timed right-hand hook against his jaw.

Howler went down. He sat on the floor shaking his head, trying to clear the swarm of bees that seemed to have taken up residence there. He could see the faces in the sutler's doorway, the blue uniforms, the bulk of Sergeant Pierce, and directly above him, the tall man.

A hand stretched out, jerked Howler to his feet, and slammed him back against the wall. Howler screamed with anger and frustration and fought back, his arms becoming fisted windmills.

He threw lefts and rights without science, with all of his strength behind each blow. His mouth was wide open, gasping for breath. He hit nothing. Nothing at all, and the tears started to flow.

Blood trickled from his mouth, from his wide nostrils. The tall man hammered away at him methodically, breaking him as Howler struck back futilely. He went down again, felt the sickness in his gut, the weakness in his limbs. He tried to get to hands and knees, and briefly achieved it before it all went out of him and he caved in, his face smashing against the floor.

If Howler had been alert enough to hear, he would have heard the cheer go up from the soldiers gathered around the door to the sutler's store. His thoughts, unfortunately, had had a dark velvet curtain drawn over them, and he neither heard nor saw nor felt anything of this world. He lay peacefully against the rough wooden floor, a thin stream of blood still flowing from his split and battered nose.

"Jesus," First Sergeant Pierce sighed. The colonel, wherever he was at present, seeing the scores of half-dressed men, the romping horses, the destruction of the grub hall, the crowd at the sutler's, must have already known what had happened, but there was a chance he did not know.

Pierce turned to the man beside him. "Corporal Stone," he said, "find Colonel MacEnroe—tell him Ruff Justice is back."